THE RIGHT OF WAY

The First In A Modern Trilogy

THE RIGHT OF WAY

L.B. LEWIS

This is a work of fiction. Names, businesses, characters, places, and incidents are the products of the author's imagination or are used fictitiously. Any resemblance to actual events, locales, or persons, living or dead, is entirely coincidental.

THE RIGHT OF WAY

Cover by Elizabeth Griffin

ISBN 978-0-9978928-1-9 (Paperback)
ISBN 978-0-9978928-0-2 (E-Book)

http://www.lblewis.com

CONTENTS

Chapter 1
No Pot To Piss In

"Everyone knows you don't have a pot to piss in," my mother says, "but I don't tell them how bad it really is."

"I'm trying to get a job, Mom, and I could use your support. It's not easy for my generation," I said, trying to scrape the mold off the mozzarella I found in my fridge.

"Honestly, everyone knows because you never send gifts for your cousins' weddings or the baby showers. And everyone asks me if you have a boyfriend and when you're getting married. You should freeze your eggs. Why don't you just move back home and get a job here in Detroit? It's like you don't even think about us and we're your family." Her words are now hitting a nerve.

"Mom, I'm going to hang up the phone to try to find that pot to piss in, OK?" I said as I hit "End Call."

My new lifestyle post-MBA wasn't going over well with my parents, and lately, every phone call, like today's, was a tightrope balancing act. To try to justify my decision again to get my MBA or attempt to explain why I didn't have a job to my mother was pointless since the emotional currency of our family was finance, not feelings. What's more is, she didn't know how far in debt I was, and even I was losing track of how much I owed.

I missed my parents, and I wanted a healthy relationship with them that did not revolve around my lack of money. I was confused as to why they didn't help me by telling me what the real world would be like. They would always say that if I had to move back home as a grownup, I would need to pay them rent. I knew it was their way of encouraging me to be self-sufficient. But I was so broke and in debt now, the money I borrowed from my parents paid my rent, and I didn't have to deal with living under their roof. Under all the tension about finances, I know they missed me, which added to their filial disappointment in some way because now they were paying me to stay away from them instead of me paying rent to see them.

Coming from a conservative, upper-middle-class family where my father was lead engineer at a car parts factory and my mother didn't have to work, my younger sister Lexie and I grew up comfortably in a big house just outside of Detroit. Dad was the typical introverted engineer who didn't say much while my mom was outspoken and focused on family, food, and who I was going to marry. She wanted desperately for me or my sister to marry some Italian man who was Catholic so she could reconnect with her lost roots.

I knew I needed to hang up before she asked again how my Italian ex-boyfriend Matteo was and if we would ever get back together. Marriage was the solution to her own problems, which she projected onto my sister and me along with the Midwestern values of integrity, honesty, and working hard. Although my father was the cornerstone of her life, and they still loved each other very much after twenty-eight years of marriage, I thought sometimes by looking at my parents that their marriage was just co-dependency inertia and I never wanted that.

Besides, I thought, marriage was something I would do after I was established. I wanted something different in my life than the women in my family. I chose to make my career my top priority by pursuing my MBA and moving from Detroit to Washington, D.C., three years ago.

Everything seemed more hopeful when I arrived in D.C., even though the plumbing had a small issue and the back patio to my new basement apartment in Glover Park was covered with raw sewage the day my mom was helping me move in. Tired from the car ride and appalled that her daughter chose to live in a basement and, now, a basement that smelled like sewage, she went up the stairs to the back door, knocked, and after a few pleasantries blasted my new landlord with, "Listen, I don't care if you are some kind of lawyer, get your ass in gear and clean up your shit so my daughter doesn't have to live like this."

It was just like her then and today to be offensive to get her point across. The last thing I needed was to know that *everyone* in my conservative family was passing judgment on me because I was an unemployed, single woman living in a basement with my MBA and although I had a toilet, I couldn't afford a pot to piss in that was acceptable.

The bright future post-MBA that was sold to me was paid for in loans and left me incredibly in debt. Emotionally, I was numb. I kept on applying for jobs online and going to networking events to sell myself to get a foot in the door, pay my dues, work my way up. At this point, I really didn't care what job I was going to get. Settling for the mediocrity of that imaginary employee lifestyle would be one step above the emotional numbness of my current situation. Any full-time job with health benefits was all I needed.

To make ends meet, I started working part-time as a cashier at Whole Foods in March. I was one step away from moving back to my parents' house in Detroit or going on public assistance. I had not been able to pay off any of my debt and had got into more debt because I couldn't find a real job. Too afraid to apply for health insurance and unsure if I could pay for it, I also didn't have that either. I was falling through the cracks of society with an advanced degree.

Chapter 2
Stagnation

The addiction that some people have to Facebook, Instagram, or Twitter, I didn't have. I didn't have it because I didn't have a fear of missing out. It was better for me to miss out. I had deleted all my social media accounts except LinkedIn because I needed that for looking for jobs. I was afraid of knowing, and I was afraid of being judged by my successful friends and *everyone* in my family circle. To see all the happy pictures of friends and frenemies celebrating their new jobs, weddings, or trips left me sad, depressed and lonely. The more I tried to keep up by posting awkward photos the more I saw myself trying to fake it until I made it exclusively for external validation purposes, which got to be so unbearable, even I couldn't stand it.

My good friend Jennifer and I still kept in somewhat regular contact even without me using social media. She had more student loans than I did and one maxed-out co-signed credit card as we broke some societal taboo by talking about our debt when I was in business school and she was in law school. We were both staunch supporters of women's rights and well aware that the gender pay gap still existed, thanks in part to our mothers' generation. To compensate for inequality, Jennifer and I rotated happy hours at different bars in Dupont Circle to see if we would get a guy to buy us drinks since we were both so broke.

When Jennifer graduated from law school, she was interviewing for a few jobs in D.C. and San Francisco. Her father, an accomplished partner in a corporate law firm, sat down with her to discuss all the offers she ended up receiving. She really wanted to work in immigration and family law and continue with the small firm she interned with in San Francisco, but she knew that this job would not pay her bills and confided in me that she didn't want to disappoint her father, since she also received an offer to join his firm. In a twist of fate, her father asked her, deep down, what she would like to do with her life. The heavy burden of trying to please him, pay her loans, and thinking about the future resulted in Jennifer not speaking. Her father kept on talking about stability, hard work, and paying her dues, until she found the courage to interrupt and say, "Dad, I want to work at a small firm and help immigrants."

From what she told me after, he looked at her and said, "You're my daughter, and I knew you were going to say that. That doesn't make me any less proud of you; in fact, it makes me more proud that you are helping others. Just like you will continue to help those people, I will help you. Forget about your loans. I will pay them all for you. Done."

I was so happy and mad at the same time when she told me about it. Supporting my friend was part of friendship. Why couldn't I share in her happiness? Why was I upset and jealous of her? Maybe because my father didn't offer to do something like that, partially because we didn't have the same tax bracket as Jennifer's family. But also, sometimes, the idea of helping others was foreign to my family members.

And, realistically, while people in my networks were employed, having kids, and collecting pictures of fancy food porn, there was no way I was going to start posting about saving 70 percent of my grocery bill. Because I was so in debt, I had to find ways to get by, so, I started practicing the art of extreme frugality. I learned how to be cheap by reading online articles like "How to Pay off Your Debt" and by watching *Extreme Cheapskates*.

Until I found a real job, my budget included no discretionary items, and I could only buy the necessities, usually with coupons and if the items were on sale. I could eat at work and got a discount, which is the main reason why I chose that job.

When I wasn't at work, I was dedicated to cooking my own meals and avoided going out. Dried beans instead of canned beans. Use a tea bag three times. Walk instead of driving or public transportation. If I was going to a café to use the internet, I would bring my own tea bag and just pay for the cup and water. Sometimes, I would even bring my own sandwich or cookies to eat if I was going to spend a long time there. Diluting dish soap with water was an art that didn't have to be undertaken only when there was a little remaining, as I did it before using any to stretch one bottle to three.

And I would negotiate everything I could to be a lower price. I would always attempt to get the damage discount at clothing stores, like that winter coat I got at Marshalls which had a microscopic ink stain on the inside. More recently, I even tried to negotiate at Kinko's when my resume printed out in color instead of black and white. I liked the art of negotiating in business and felt that this was all good practice for a real job.

About six months after graduation, my frustration level got to be so high that I started experimenting with marking different ethnic categories on job applications. I wanted to see if I might have a better chance for an interview or a job if I self-identified as a Pacific Islander, Hispanic, or African-American descendent. My friends had pointed out numerous times that I was so ethnically ambiguous with my brown curly hair, light skin and dark brown eyes I could pass for something more exotic than my English, Polish, and Italian roots. And, since I minored in Spanish and my name was Sierra, some people incorrectly assumed that I must be Hispanic. Besides, I thought it didn't really matter what I put down because I had yet to find a company that asked for genetic testing in addition to a background check and drug screening. But, in this experiment, the end goal was a job, and that had not manifested itself no matter what box I checked.

I had gotten to the point where I would expect a rejection email within one week of applying for a job. It was a sort of game I played where I would print out the rejection emails. I also kept an Excel spreadsheet of the personal or the robot email address that sent the rejection email to me with the date in a separate column. I did this to keep my Excel skills sharp and, if I felt like it, to follow up with that person about future opportunities.

And, now after ending the call with my mother, I was still pondering the numbness. In light of Jennifer's situation, I thought that the world is an unequal place, especially if you have a lot of debt. I also knew somewhere deep down that I had to try. I would write a follow-up email to the phone interview I had last week for a firm called Brown and White in Houston. It was a shot in the dark to try to get any job, with my confidence low, inability to make decisions, and borderline obsessive compulsive cheapness feeding my free time. My life was so pathetic, and I had no clear idea of when *everyone* would approve of me, including me.

Chapter 3
Next Stop: Houston

It had been two weeks since I had the last disturbing call with my mother when I got an email back from Brown and White requesting another phone interview. The email said that this time I would be speaking with the hiring manager, Roberto, or "Bob" as he was known. I responded and accepted the invitation for the second round interview.

I had heard about Brown and White from a classmate's mass email. Job openings were never posted on their site and applicants could only be considered if they had some type of referral. All the entry-level analyst jobs were customized to the applicant's skills, so the email said. I sent a reply to his mass email and I attached my resume. Within a day, my classmate said he referred me but I'm not sure how he knew someone there or what the referral had said because I didn't really know that classmate. It was just one of the random job applications I had done hoping that it would pay off even though I wasn't even sure what the job really was about or if I was qualified.

The day came for the interview and I sat down next to the small window of my basement apartment so that I would have the best reception. When the 713 area code showed up on the phone, I waited until the third ring to answer it.

"Hello. This is Sierra," I said, standing up to give some power to my voice. I was wearing high heels and my pajamas to make a statement of power and comfort.

"Hi, Sierra. This is Bob, from Brown and White, all the way from Houston. Listen, I don't really like phone interviews that much so what do you say if you just tell me a few sentences about yourself and why you want this job."

"OK. I'm Sierra Wellington and I graduated with my MBA last year with a concentration in real estate. I'd like this job to build my experience with a known firm and to work with a team."

"Do you know where Houston is? I'm sure you do. But why do you want to move to Houston?"

"I think it would be a new experience and I'm open to relocation."

"Thanks, Sierra. We'll be in touch about next steps."

"Thank you, Bob." And, with that, I hung up the phone to realize that the conversation lasted three minutes and twenty-three seconds. Everything in the job search to date was unpredictable and I just figured that since the call was so short with only two questions that it probably was just out of courtesy before they sent me a rejection email. I couldn't imagine what the next step would be after such a short phone interview, but I wrote a thank you email to my contact in Human Resources anyway that I closed with "I look forward to learning more about this opportunity."

I looked forward to learning more about any opportunity that would pay me. As I closed my laptop, the pile of unopened student loan statements from Navient fell from my desk to the floor. I knew I had to do something with those and get the courage to handle my financial situation. But, I just avoided it all, stacked up the notices again and told myself this weekend I would have to organize them.

Next week was June already and it marked thirteen months I had been out of school and looking for a job. I had negotiated hard with my landlord to let me stay until I found a job. He gave me until August when I would have to move out because he only wanted to rent to current students.

Even though he gave me until August, I had barely enough to pay for June's rent and thought about getting another part-time job. Summer would be a good time to find some fun, seasonal work because I heard companies don't hire for full-time roles in the summer since many of their employees go on vacation. In reality, I had two job searches going on: one for a fun seasonal job and one for a real nine-to-five job.

On my way to work on June 1st, I mailed my rent check and ended up a few minutes late. I didn't think anything of it as I punched in under the five minute mark. Everything was fine I thought until I got a note on my time card that said "Late Warning." I was over this job and the warnings. I took my lunch to sit outside and noticed I had a missed call from a 713 number. I checked my email and got a message from Brown and White thanking me for my interest in the job and then inviting me to Houston next week to meet the team.

Staring at my phone for a few seconds I then closed out of my email and finished eating my lunch. By the time I got back into Whole Foods and punched in, I had already mentally decided to think about the job for the remainder of my shift and write the Houston office an email when I got home as to not appear too eager.

Obviously, this was a good sign that they are flying me down to Houston to meet the team. And, it was a good sign that it was moving fast because I didn't have time to waste. But, I really didn't know anything about Houston. D.C. was the most south of the Mason-Dixon line I had ever been, not counting Disneyworld. I knew I didn't have a real choice and I had to start getting some income. I wrote Houston back and waited for my eTicket and hotel confirmation to be sent. I would spend three days, two nights in Houston and also would meet with a real estate agent that helped with rentals.

One thing I couldn't remember was what ethnicity I had put down in the preliminary questionnaires so I had to pretend to be anything and be prepared for any politically incorrect question like the one time a Human Resources manager asked me point blank if I was black because I was from Detroit. Or the other time, during a phone screening, the interviewer asked me if I was from Mexico and if I knew what my name meant in Spanish. While I thought these questions were illegal, I kept on playing the game and learned to adapt to people's need for bucketization.

Before I knew it I was on my way to Houston for the job interview. The three hour flight gave me time to focus and think about what I was going to say. It also gave me time to negotiate with myself why I needed to put myself out there for the sake of being a part of the working class that was some sort of rite of passage. Even though working in my first job out of business school in a city I had never visited was out of my comfort zone, almost like a second puberty, this was what I thought was supposed to happen.

As the plane landed at Hobby Airport, I grabbed the arm rests so hard I know I had white knuckles. But, I didn't look at my hands because I was too busy having an anxiety attack while staring at the back of the seat in front of me, as my heart pounded out palpitations. Desperate was an understatement. My mind was already five steps ahead and I decided that I was going to take the job in Houston no matter what. I had to stop waiting for something to happen and make it happen. My debts were compounding interest every second. This was it.

Chapter 4
Messing With Texas

The interview trip to Houston was a blur. I remember seeing a driver that had a sign with "Sierra Wellington" waiting for me after I grabbed my suitcase off the baggage claim carousel. We soon left the airport and drove into a sprawling urban metropolis that I later learned was called the "Loop" with block after block of large skyscrapers mixed with other smaller buildings. Something was so unfamiliar and unsettling about the aesthetic chaos of this un-zoned landscape.

Then, the driver pulled up to a dated 1980's style, dark windowed mid-rise building that had a sign out in front for Brown and White. Showtime, I thought, as my stomach churned. Everything was moving in slow motion when I stepped out of the sedan into the hot, humid air and walked with heavy legs to the door.

Once in the office, I remember vaguely meeting a secretary and who showed me the way to the conference room called Crockett. Then, she asked, "Would you like something to drink? We have coffee, water, coke."

"I'll take a Coke, please."

"OK, what kind?"

"A Coke, please."

"You'd like a Coca-Cola, hon?"

"Yes, thank you."

What was so difficult about asking for a pop, I thought. I was confused as to why she asked me what kind of coke I wanted and thought maybe it was because they had Coke Zero or Cherry Coke or something else.

For the duration of the two day interview process, I sat in the same seat at a conference table drinking Coca-Cola. There were about seven men that came into the room to talk with me, including the hiring manager, Bob, whom previously interviewed me over the phone. Meeting him in person was a bit of a surprise as I soon realized how old his picture on the website really was. Bob was in his late-forties, balding with a comb-over, about sixty pounds overweight and stood only a hair taller than myself, probably about 5'7. I learned that he was originally from Texas, with his parents migrating to Houston from Puebla and had built up his career in hospitality in Texas and Mexico.

I also met Greg, who was on Bob's team. Like Bob, Greg was also on the shorter side and was about the same height as me. He had sandy brown hair, a stocky build and noticeably short arms. Greg was five years my senior and was from Austin. He graduated from Texas A&M and moved to Houston when he received an offer to join Brown and White after he met Bob at an on-campus recruiting event.

During all the interviews, I was learning a little more about the job responsibilities as an analyst.

I found out I had to travel at times to do market research for clients that contracted Brown and White to do feasibility studies. I also would have to produce reports for Brown and White associates as well as for their clients. But, I wasn't sure how to ask if I would be working with any women and I thought it was strange that I didn't meet any yet except a secretary.

By the end of day two in the conference room, I was exhausted. The morning of the third day, before my plane flew out, I had coffee with another one of the secretaries. The secretary was nice enough and we had a chat about how hot Houston can get in the summer. I then asked her if any other women worked at Brown and White. She mentioned a director named Pamela who was traveling and how Greg had a crush on her. Then, the cat was out of the gossip bag and she also mentioned that there was a rumor that Bob owned a chain of taquerias in Mexico somewhere and that he wasn't the same since his divorce a few years ago.

The coffee meeting didn't last more than twenty minutes before a real estate agent showed up and took me to see three apartments. I decided to fill out an application for a one-bedroom a few blocks from the office and had the company pay for the application fee, as the secretary told me they had a working relationship with this agent.

Within one week, the offer letter came in the mail with a start date of August 1st. Accepting this job in the Lone Star State seemed like the right thing to do to get completely off my parent's payroll and start to pay down my growing credit card and student loan debt. I didn't really care what the salary was because I just knew I had to negotiate partly because I was a woman who wanted to be paid fairly and partly because I needed all I could get including a relocation bonus. By the time I did negotiate all moving fees to be covered by the company and a salary increase of five thousand dollars, I felt that I was now on a path to financial independence.

After the final offer letter was signed and returned, it was already July. The announcement of my new southern trajectory was met with apathy by my family and close friends. While I thought the same everyone would suddenly be happy for me, there wasn't much emotion or commentary either way. I really was deep down looking for some kind of social media-type thumbs up approval after fourteen months of treading water and struggling to find a job. But, people were more excited about telling me their summer vacation plans than listening about my life change. No one had even offered to help me pack and move which made the company hired movers the only ones that seemed to care about my stuff at least, and they were getting paid.

Chapter 5
Hot and Bothered

I landed in Houston on Thursday, July 28th and spent the weekend at another forgettable, chain hotel near the office right across the street from the hotel I stayed at during the interview process. My first day was Monday, August 1st and I could also get the keys to my new apartment then. I had a rental car that the company paid for one month and could also walk to work from the hotel.

Monday finally arrived. I had received an email on Friday welcoming me and letting me know that I could come to the office at 10:00 am on my first day. I took my time getting ready and wore the same suit I interviewed in for this momentous day. After checking out of the hotel, I took my suitcases to the rental car where I'd keep them until I went to my apartment after work.

As I entered the office, I was first greeted by a secretary I hadn't met before.

"Hi, I'm Clara. Welcome to the office! I'm fixin' to get you all set up. Where are you from?" she asked as she took my new computer from the box and handed it to me along with a phone list, Wi-Fi code list and map of the office.

"Originally, from Michigan but spent the last few years on the East Coast," I said, excited and nervous, not only to use this new MacBook but also to finally have a real job with a real paycheck.

"A Yankee. Well, you might feel relieved that we don't get any of that white stuff down here in Houston," she snorted out a laugh and then answered the phone.

Trying hard to not to be rude as I didn't want to eavesdrop on the conversation, I walked away from her desk and into a cubical wall on accident. I noticed this cubical had my name on it literally so it didn't really matter. I sat down with my new computer and started to set it up. It had been a while since I used a MacBook and after I connected to the internet, I took a look at the online manual. I was concentrating so hard on making sure all my settings were exactly how I wanted them.

"Welcome, Sierra. Ready for lunch?" brought me back to the office environment and I saw Bob's head pop over the same wall I crashed into minutes earlier.

"Oh yes, that sounds great."

It was barely 11:30 am and my new colleagues were already waiting for me by the door, ready to go to Papi's Tex-Mex restaurant.

"You're gonna love Papi's! Everyone loves the guac," said Greg, sounding a bit too excited.

There was no avoiding the traditional first day lunch that was some type of corporate bonding ritual that I never will understand. I was nervous to begin with coupled with the fact that I strongly disliked eating in front of people, namely my coworkers, to the point that I would eat in my car on occasions to avoid having to go out to lunch. There was no hiding in my car this time. I reminded myself I had to do it, at least once, with this team, and, after all, this lunch was on the company and I couldn't do anything weird because I needed to make a good impression.

"I love guac and chips," I replied to Greg who was now walking by my side to Papi's.

"Do they have Tex-Mex in Michigan?" he asked.

"Of course, there are Mexican restaurants in Michigan and in D.C., too. That's where I was living before I took this job."

I didn't really want to ask what made "Tex-Mex" different from the Mexican food I had eaten before moving to Houston. The good thing was at this point in the conversation, no one seemed to care about what I said anyway because we were about to enter Papi's.

Papi's looked like it used to be a Chinese restaurant with some leftover gold characters on the wall of our private room. And, for some reason they put balloons around the table for six and even had a piñata donkey hanging from the seventies light fixture. Greg stuck close to me and took the seat next to mine.

As if on command, our server, Angela, brought out two huge bowls of guacamole and chips only seconds after we arrived and let us know that the air conditioning was broke. It didn't matter to our group as Greg was not shy about grabbing one bowl and put it in between us. Then, he grabbed a basket of chips and put it next to our bowl of guacamole. After a few chips, he paused and asked me, "So, what made you take this job?"

I sat there and felt a pang of anxiety in my chest as I looked up and saw all five faces stop crunching on their chips and look at me. Being the only woman at the table was now making me feel like the piñata donkey knowing each question was like the swing of a bat. And this game would go further and further until they were satisfied in "figuring me out" and able to categorize me. Was I cute enough? Was I smart enough? I thought perhaps I might explode if this continued too long, just like the piñata after being hit enough times. Gathering myself on the inside and reciting something my veteran great uncle used to say before there was that popular deodorant commercial: "Never let them see you sweat." But today, with the air conditioning not working, everyone was seeing me sweat adding to my physical and mental discomfort.

"Oh, Greg, I really enjoyed our conversation during the interview process and saw this as the right opportunity at the right time," I said slowly and confidently with a flirty, bitchy smile and a look in all directions to send a warning, "I am cute and I am smart, even if I have sweat pouring out of body."

Then, Angela reappeared and we all were asked what we would like. It was amazing that after Bob ordered everyone ordered the same thing: a cheese chimichanga. I didn't want a cheese chimichanga so I ordered the enchiladas which the menu said were the house specialty.

"Why didn't you order the cheese chimichanga? It's the best and we all love it," Bob said.

"Oh, next time. I wanted to try the house specialty," I replied cordially.

The rest of the lunch was surprisingly mellow with everyone very much focused on eating their chimichangas without any more questions directed at me. All five present almost licked their plates as they were spotless when Angela came to clear them. No one ordered dessert or coffee and we walked back to the office.

When we got back to the office in lethargy mode, too full of food to do any real work, Bob gave me a thick company manual and said "Read this." So, I sat at my desk concentrating on the company history, business units and office locations. While reading the manual, I felt very proud to be working for Brown and White, a company with such a long, successful history and global reach. I felt that finally my four years of undergraduate education and two years earning my MBA was worth it. My educational fulfillment in that moment was at an all-time high as I read about the quintessential American Dream story of two hardworking business partners who succeeded in building their empire by assisting other businesses. I wanted to be like them, to carry on their tradition of excellence in business. I so desperately wanted to succeed, learn, and earn a paycheck to help me be a contributing member of society. I wanted to flaunt Brown and White's name on LinkedIn, in my alumni database and on conference badges. Maybe in two years I could be a director if I really worked hard, I thought. And, if I did well enough, in like five years, I could retire.

This daydream full of ambitions abruptly ended with a text message notification on my phone. I knew I shouldn't check my phone during work or look at sites that were on the list of sites to avoid. Apparently, this company blocked any site that was thought to be a social network or offensive and the manual also said that there was a program installed to monitor my productivity. This was something new to me and I wondered what websites were going to be blocked. It didn't matter because I was determined to succeed here and was going to do whatever it took.

A further jolt back to reality was the section "Disciplinary Actions." It never occurred to me that I would not do a good job in this position. I had to do a good job here; I had no choice. After all, I am very intelligent and a quick learner, as I told them in my interview. I had asked my references, all of whom were former professors of mine, to stress this fact because I knew I didn't have that much work experience. I also am a people person and I like working in teams.

The cliché interview rhetoric that landed me this job was the truth, or so I pretended it was. After fifteen months of not working after my MBA, I knew that if I did not succeed here I would have a credit catastrophe, default on my loans and probably end up trying to get paid to talk about an ebook I wrote on Dr. Phil about how having your MBA doesn't mean having it all or something lame like that.

"So, what do you think of your new company, Sierra?" asked Bob as he stood near the entrance to my cubicle.

"I'm definitely excited to be here and can't wait to start on my first project!" I replied with genuine enthusiasm.

"Well, you'll be drinking water from a fire hose soon enough. Why don't you call it day and we'll see you tomorrow, OK?"

"Thanks, Bob. Have a good day, I mean night, and we'll see you tomorrow."

I shut my computer down and placed it in my desk drawer. I took my key out to lock the door when Greg popped his head over the cubicle wall.

"You coming back tomorrow, Sierra?" he asked with a smile.

"I think so. Have a good night," I replied returning his smile.

I finished locking the drawer and thought Greg must be incredibly friendly or just trying following some blog's suggestions on how to make a new person feel welcome. It was nice but also creepy that he's so dedicated almost like an emotional support dog. I quickly walked out of the office and got into my car. I looked over my shoulder to see if Greg was nearby and to my relief, he was nowhere in sight.

Chapter 6
Fitting In [My Pants]

After work, I stopped by Target to get an air mattress and then headed to my new apartment. I picked up my keys and was surprised to already have some mail waiting for me including my relocation check. Wow, I'm so excited to be here and work for Brown and White, I thought as I held the check in my hand.

I immediately went up to my apartment which was on the third floor. I hadn't seen it when I came down for my interview trip because it wasn't vacant then. It was close to 700 sq. feet with wall-to-wall carpeting, electric stove, microwave, full bath, and a balcony that looked over the pool. It smelled freshly painted and there was a fruit basked waiting for me with a card that said, "Welcome Home, Sierra." I took a seat on the counter and looked at the fruit basket filled with apples, oranges and pears. I opened the card that it came with and found out it was from the apartment building management and thought finally I've made it. I have a real job and I don't live in a basement anymore.

This was progress that I had to document and I took a picture of the basket to send to a few people. I was really proud of the basket. Then, with my bank's app I quickly snapped the front and the back of the check and was done depositing it. Although, it would take two to three business days for the funds to be available, this money would be transferred immediately to start to make a payment on my student loans which recently had the discretionary forbearance status lifted due to previous unemployment. Since I now had a job, I had to start making the full payments and I could not mess up my financial status again.

After depositing my check, I moved into my apartment with my two suitcases and a newly acquired air mattress. It would be about a week before my stuff arrived from D.C. so I had to make the best of this air mattress and indoor camping lifestyle for now. Too exhausted to leave the apartment after the long day, I took out my new journal. A journal would keep me sane and be a good outlet for the ups and downs of this transition, I was told.

I had a feeling that the year would have many ups and downs, especially since my learning and socialization curve seemed to be steeper than previously thought, working in an all-male environment. Admittedly, I knew very little about Houston as a city or its culture. However, there could be many areas of professional opportunity, I wrote. During my interview process, I was told that I could stay a year in Houston and then be able to transfer to any other office. I didn't want to get too vested in Houston since I knew I wanted to go back to D.C. Texas was too far away from everything.

The first couple of weeks at the job were uneventful meetings and research projects. My things arrived from the moving company and I started to feel more at home. And, I began to learn a more about Houston from my colleagues and searching online during slow days. I learned that the CFO carried a gun and shot at the neighbor's dog one day while eavesdropping. When someone at work mentioned, Frito Pie I had to Google it to see how in the world Fritos could go from the bag into a pan to be baked into a pie with who knows what kind of filling. Google's answer to my question was a YouTube video called "The Texas Way: Faith, Freedom, and Frito Pies," which was almost like a documentary that highlighted Christian values, the right to bear arms and state delicacies like Frito Pie and BBQ.

And through these research projects that helped fill in my cultural understanding of Houston, it was not a surprise to me to learn that Houston was considered to be one of America's Fattest Cities. It is true from my humble observations that everything was bigger in Texas, even the people and their pets. Someone told me that Houston also has a very high restaurant to people ratio which could explain something.

I also noticed that many women I had come in contact appeared to be anorexic, had a large amount of plastic surgery or were overweight. Women wore a lot more makeup here than what I'd been used to. And, as if it was out of some sci-fi clone movie, the vast majority of women had highlights or dyed blonde hair in some long-layered fashion. Even men, Indian men included, had blonde highlights.

It did not appeal to me whatsoever to be like the majority of Houstonites I saw. I tried to eat healthy and save money by bringing salads to the office. I did, however, need to find a gym soon or my butt would be an office ass just like Greg's. Greg's office ass fit perfectly into his desk chair as if it was custom made for his padded backside.

Since it was early August, I decided to come up with a goal per month, kind of like a New Year's Resolution. August's goal was to join a gym. There was a small gym close by my apartment and thought that would be a good place to start. Although the gym was geared towards overweight women, they offered a number of classes which is what I really wanted to do to slim down. I didn't really care about losing weight, I just wanted to fit into my black skinny jeans again and be proactive about not growing into my desk chair.

When I walked into the gym, I saw a few overweight ladies bouncing on trampolines and then saw them going to another station to do various free weights. There was a husky looking woman with a Longhorn t-shirt on marching in front of a television in the middle of the trampolines and cardio equipment. I wanted to look at what her workout consisted of but didn't want to stare.

Near the far right of the gym, about five feet away from the cardio class in front of the TV was a desk with another plump woman sitting at a computer. I politely asked about the yoga class that I saw on their website. She handed me a release form to fill out on a clipboard and told me that the class would begin when the woman who was marching was finished with her DVD. The class consisted of the gym trainer putting in a DVD for me to watch. I was too embarrassed to leave and needed some stress relief so I filled out the form and did the yoga DVD for the ladies on the trampolines to see.

After my special yoga DVD was finished, I was invited to a potluck and also was encouraged to take advantage of their no initiation dues offer. I was also offered gym gear and supplements to meet my goals faster. While the offer was tempting and everyone was friendly, I felt the urge to get in my car as soon as humanly possible. I had my own DVD player at home. The finding-a-gym goal was now on hold.

Chapter 7
Dating On Demand

In business school, I had heard that there were two out of three areas one could be good at in life: work, family and friends. My family and friends were far away and I had been focused on getting a job and now working hard. After the discouraging gym experiment, September's goal would be to meet new people. I really wanted to make some friends, maybe learn about a gym from them and date a nice guy. It had been so long since I had met a new friend to go to happy hours with and even longer since I went on a date.

Per the recommendation of Jennifer, who was Jewish, I posted a profile on JDate. She made that suggestion in response to my complaints that I wasn't meeting any sophisticated guys in Houston and I was too scared to try Tinder. Since she had been using the JDate app she told me that she had already gone out with a few guys who were smart, successful and polite.

This made perfect sense since I had the goal of meeting men who had similar interests and aspirations like me. I clearly put on my profile I was not Jewish and had no interest in converting. I wasn't interested in a hook-up or something serious. Plus, I didn't put a picture on my profile and I was OK with guys not having pictures, either. I honestly wanted to meet quality, successful men and I thought perhaps online dating could be a great way to choose who I would meet to do something noncommittal and in a low stress way.

In reality, it turned out to be more a life lesson than I bargained for. My first and last experience on the site was with a guy named Noah. I didn't see what he looked like but when he had called me to finalize plans I could tell that Noah was on the larger side or a smoker by his slightly raspy voice. During our short call, he told me how hard it was to be Jewish and single in Houston. I didn't doubt him; I knew it was hard to even breathe sometimes in humid and superficial Houston let alone talk to someone. We made plans for later in the week to meet at an Italian restaurant that he said was his favorite.

When I arrived at the restaurant, I saw an obese man in a long black t-shirt, gold chain and denim shorts standing near the front door. I didn't really care what he looked like since I was going out to a new place and thought he could be a nice guy.

"Hi Noah," I said and put out my hand.

"Oh, my God. You're gorgeous," he said as he looked me up and down and sideways. He took my hand and put it on some part of his sweaty back and then kissed my right cheek.

"Thanks; shall we go in?" I sputtered out nervously because all of a sudden my hope of this being friendly had taken a different turn and my hand was now damp from his back.

Once in the restaurant, we sat down in a corner booth. He then carried on about heartless girls who didn't like him and to his astuteness, he thought it was because he was overweight. This led to the question: "So, do you think I'm attractive?" I guess him kissing me and now this question was him taking things to the next level which made me uncomfortable and I tried to focus on my delicious lobster ravioli. My brain was turning over possible things to say like "I'm sure someone finds you attractive, but it's not me." I politely put this as "Yes, you'll meet someone who finds you attractive in the way you'd like to be thought of."

While the meal itself was great, the night's conversation began to get awkward and included a lot of depressing stories. It was Noah's idea to go to an international club after dinner where he knew a bartender. The club played good music and we sat down next to a group of well dressed, twenty-something Houstonites. For a moment, I vicariously was part of their group. They all seemed to be having fun and enjoying each other's company.

Then, I looked over to who I came with. Noah asked me what I was doing in the coming week. I said it was my birthday and I started to cry. I was crying for myself at this point, because I knew I would be alone or working late. He tried to be helpful and said, "I could spend your birthday with you," at which point, I began to cry uncontrollably, and he put his hand on my leg. As if his hand was a giant, Texas-sized fly, I swatted it off my leg and returned it back to his leg.

I was in a difficult state of depressive mind and didn't think the suggestion of Noah spending my birthday with me was something that was going to turn this around. I tried to explain to him what I was going through with my transition. He attempted to be helpful and share a very tragic personal story involving the death of someone close to him. It made me even more depressed and I suggested that we leave.

That night, I decided to pull my profile off that dating site. I didn't want to give it a second chance as maybe I didn't understand what Jewish culture was about in Houston. I texted Jennifer that I broke up with JDate and was never going back. As a replacement for JDate, I tried a free app a few weeks later and decided to meet an Egyptian expat for dinner. I thought it could be exotic to meet a man from Egypt who was in Houston working for an oil and gas company.

We went to dinner at Papi's because he asked me to suggest a place and that was the only place I could think of. When he arrived, I discovered he spoke very limited English in short phrases. What was funny was that even though he said he was head of his division in his online profile, I began to wonder if that was true. I honestly couldn't comprehend anything he was saying. Even stranger was that he went to the bathroom when the check came and I ended up paying for the dinner just to leave as soon as possible. After our server came back with my change, he reappeared with his phone out and said, "Photo?" to which I said, "Nope" and walked towards my car to leave him still in Papi's, holding his phone.

Dismal thoughts of the future and why my two meetings with men from the internet weren't even fun were occupying my attention during my drive home. Sure, there were other men that had messaged me but for some reason I chose two losers to waste my time on. I was alone and had one out of the three important things in my life: my job. Looking away from the road for just a second to read a billboard that said, "We clean up suicides so you don't have to," I almost rear-ended the car in front of me. My car was stopped in the middle of the road for who knows how long until a police car came up alongside of me and the officer asked, "Is everything alright, Miss?"

"No, I mean yes, officer. Thanks." I stepped on the gas and somehow found my way back to my apartment.

Chapter 8
Mentoring 101

The next day turned into the next month and before I knew it, it was the end of September. My birthday had passed just as another day. The exception was a few phone calls and cards from family and friends. I was relieved that no one at the office knew.

I was now to start Brown and White's mentorship program. This would begin with my formal introduction to Pamela, my assigned mentor. She had been traveling for a client the last two months and I had only seen her a few times in the office. As I learned during my chat with the secretary, who no longer worked at Brown and White, Pamela was one of the very few women in the company who achieved a standing higher than secretary after being there twenty some years. Perhaps her tenure was in part to her reputation as the office cougar. The funny thing was that Pamela was not your average, as seen on TV cougar. Pamela was approximately fifty-five years old, graying hair highlighted streaky blond, average height with an average American size twelve body with no style or sophistication. Although she had two kids, she had never been married and never had brought anyone to a Christmas party, so the gossip said.

When I first learned that she would be my mentor, I cringed inside. I thought any woman that wears a navy fleece jacket with wide-legged khakis and black patent leather stiletto heels will remain single until eternity. She looked like a homely, suburban cougar mom trying to elongate her wide, stout legs and seem sexy in an inappropriate, mismatched way. Or maybe those khakis were really tear-away stripper pants for seducing young men so the heels would make sense. But, I reminded myself she is not my style mentor but my professional mentor. My external judgment of her fashion sense had nothing to do with her ability to do her job.

We met in her office after I was formally introduced to her as her mentee by Bob. I noticed that her office was in the far corner and also had fresh cut flowers near a picture frame of her and her kids.

"Nice flowers," I said, thinking a compliment would break the ice.

"Oh, thanks," She said nonchalantly as she sat down and whipped her head to the right so that the hair was out of her eyes.

"Now, Sierra, I wanted to check in with you to see how everything is going and also talk to you about some upcoming projects we have for you to start."

"Well, everything is fine. I've started the research for the San Antonio shopping center project and, I think, I could handle some more projects."

"Oh, your references were right. You are an eager beaver!"

Her phone started to ring and she quickly said, "We'll have to talk more next week during dinner. I'll send you an invite."

I stood up and walked out of her office and sat back at my desk. Sure enough, the invite already arrived and I had no choice but to accept it. It was for next Tuesday at Tia's, another Tex-Mex place. I guess they call it Tex-Mex for a reason, as these places seemed to multiply in shopping centers, filled with Texans, Mexicans and Tex-Mexicans with all you can eat chips and salsa.

Tia's was a step below Papi's and was part of a chain that only got three stars on Yelp. Pamela tried to be cordial, but I felt like a fish out of water, not for lack of confidence, but knowing that all the strained small talk was a just a façade. I had quickly learned in my outings with members of the company that it is important to try to impress others by asking for top-shelf anything and always valet park your car. In typically Houston fashion, she asked for top-shelf tequila for our five dollar sized margaritas, only to be disappointed as the waiter pointed out the swirling margarita machine back behind the bar. I sat there smiling so much so that my face actually began to hurt and it was just the first five minutes into the dinner.

"Now, Sierra, we have to do some girl talk. You know all the boys in the office want to know if you are single or taken. So, what's your status, girl?"

My heart sank into my stomach at the same time the sharp edges of a chip I just put in my mouth cut my gums. While chewing, and wondering what to say, I remembered some advice a friend told me about wearing a mental raincoat to protect against other people's shit storms that sometimes can fly on you.

This storm that was starting by my aging cougar of a mentor, Pamela, was showing signs of being very messy. She now wanted to cross a very personal and private line that was absolutely none of her business. And, how can a female colleague who is supposed to be a mentor, ask a question that almost borders on sexual harassment or possibly lead to discriminatory statements and behaviors if I did not answer this question in an anticipated, normal way defined by Pamela herself.

As if my chewing took up too much of her precious time, she continued, "I told Bob, I said, look at the way the poor girl dresses. Do you really think she is single and looking for some action? She wears only flats, faded black pants and cotton sweaters that don't show a thing. I'd put my money on it that she has at least two kids and a man at home."

And, with that, I swallowed my chip and took a long sip of water. Our mutual disdain for each other's fashion sense was now almost fully out in the open. I looked at her straight in the eye. I got the feeling that she had been rejected for a good part of her life which evolved into a heightened level of insecurity. This made it so hard for other people to like her because she did not like herself. Whether it was by her behavior that she just exhibited or her heinous fashion sense, I came to the conclusion that no decent human being could be her friend. Her cougar status also confirmed that the power she wielded was unequal and misused, but young men didn't mind the trade-off. I was the lucky prey this evening and I was trying to figure out how to be me in this strange situation.

"Pamela, was just admiring your scarf. Where did you get it?" deflecting her shit and being the prey as best I could as if I didn't even hear her question.

"Oh, it was a gift from my sister who lives in Manhattan. You know they have the best shopping in Manhattan? Speaking of shopping, I think you could use a few new things and we could go shopping on Saturday to spruce you up? Maybe get you a makeover at Bobbi Brown just so you look like you fit in the office more. You're in Houston now! And, maybe your husband will treat you better if you look better, too."

I sat there and almost barfed in my mouth. Who does she think she is? If this was not the beginning of my own personal Civil War, I don't know what is. Just because I don't wear heels and a lot of makeup doesn't make me in need of an office-sponsored makeover.

"Does that mean the company will pay for it?" I was half joking and half serious.

"Sierra, you have got to be kidding, right?"

Just then the food arrived and Pamela immediately sent back her taco salad because they did not put the sour cream on the side. My tamales arrived looking as tamales should and I watched them while we waited for another salad to arrive.

"So, you will go to Mexico in couple weeks with the team to do the new project?"

"Yes, and I can't wait. I've never been to Mexico. Brushing up on my Spanish now so that I can at least get around. I minored in Spanish but I can't really say anything. "

"Oh, don't worry about that, Sierra. You'll be with Greg and Bob. They both speak the espanolo and won't let you out of their sight."

The new taco salad finally arrived and I could eat my now cold tamales. The silence of both of us eating was a welcome relief from the previous conversations. After our plates had been cleared, Pamela made promises to go out dinner every month with me and to help me professionally and personally. She even invited me to go to a basketball game in a few months. It was finally time to leave and while walking me to my car, she said, "Think about how you look at the office, Sierra. See you tomorrow."

Chapter 9
Salsarific

The next day before work, I took a long look in the mirror. I hadn't been feeling like myself the last two months since I moved to Houston. My skin looked dull, my hair needed a cut and my triceps hung down like flags of fat. But, I had made three online loan payments to Navient already and that was worth it although truth be told, I was entering a new phase of denial about how I looked and felt. October's goal was to combine August and September's goal into dance classes in order to meet new people and burn calories. I didn't know if I was more critical of the bigger version of myself after what Pamela had said or if it was just how life as a professional is supposed to be when you have a fifty hour a week job.

I was into month three at Brown and White and was still working overtime almost every night until 7 or 8. One night, a new office cleaner saw me at my desk and he knocked on my cubicle.

"'Scuse me, miss. Do you need your trash emptied?"

I turned and saw a dark haired, uniformed, fit-looking man smiling and rolling a large trashcan.

"Hi, how are you?" I asked him smiling and happy for the conversation.

"I'm good. How are you?"

"I'm tired and ready to go home," I said handing him my waste basket.

"Yes, working late your family doesn't have a good dinner," he looked at me and laughed good-naturedly.

"Oh, I don't have a family or kids. Just moved here from D.C.," I said, thinking for a moment about my ambivalence towards the job and working late.

"If you want some time, come try salsa dancing. I teach a class at the George Bush Community Center. You can meet new people."

"Yes, I'd love that! I've always wanted to learn how to salsa dance."

"OK, we see you on Friday night at 7:00," he said as he gave me my waste basket back.

"Wait, what is your name?" I asked.

"Miguel," he replied showing me his name tag.

"I'm Sierra. Nice to meet you. Thank you for cleaning our office. See you on Friday."

"See you."

On Friday morning, I put on my new outfit I had got at the mall on Wednesday: a black cotton cardigan sweater, a sleeveless collared shirt, bigger sized skinny jeans and black leather flats. It was the first new outfit I had bought in over two years. I saw many girls around my age wearing something similar and thought I would try to fit in more so I bought it. It was practical enough so that if it was hot, the sleeveless shirt could stand on its own. Likewise, I thought this outfit was safe enough to wear to work and then go out.

At 6:30 pm, Bob had left the office but Greg was still at his desk. I had to leave by 6:45 pm to get to the salsa class. Fun was on my agenda tonight and I was getting impatient. I sat quietly at my computer and kept on looking at the weekend, five day and ten day weather forecasts to pass the time.

It was now 6:50 pm and I heard Pamela say, "Hon, are you ready?"

"Yes," Greg replied from his cubicle.

They left without even looking at me, turned off the lights and locked me in the office. Being alone in the office was a relief. Without the phones ringing, secretaries chattering and printers running, it felt peaceful. This wore off quickly when I realized I had somewhere to go. I unlocked the door from the inside and then relocked the door once I was on the other side.

When I arrived at the community center, the parking lot was so packed I had to park on a side street nearby. I heard the loud music as I locked my doors and then walked up the sidewalk to the door.

"Ten dollars," said a woman sitting at a table near the main entrance.

I handed her a ten dollar bill and went in the main hall. There were so many people there that I was lost. Some were dancing. Some were standing in the back speaking in Spanish. I felt like I was transported to another country.

Then, I saw Miguel dancing on stage with his partner, a beautiful blonde woman in a sequined professional dancer dress. They were amazing and kept in perfect timing with each other and the music that was coming from the giant subwoofers on each side of the stage.

It was obvious to me, and I'm pretty sure all the people around me, too, that I was one of the few non-Hispanic attendees this evening. My trendy outfit stood out amidst the dresses and heels. I walked around to pretend to look for someone but that ended up drawing more attention to myself and my awkwardness.

When Miguel and his partner finished their dance, his partner announced, "Now, it's your turn. Get a partner."

I saw Miguel come down off stage and start walking towards me. He was smiling a big smile and then he grabbed my right hand.

"Hola, Sierra! Let's get you dancing!" he exclaimed excitedly.

"Síííí!" I shouted out over the music.

Then, instead of dancing with Miguel, which is what I wanted to happen, he grabbed the closest man who looked to be my father's age with a full head of gray hair. The man and Miguel then exchanged some words in Spanish and Miguel said, "One moment, Sierra."

I stood there holding Miguel's hand and fiddling with my cardigan with my left hand. I looked around and saw that people were already dancing. I wanted to start dancing.

"OK, go!" Miguel shoved my hand into a large, rough, manly hand that could have used some lotion.

"Hola," I heard and I looked up to see a tall, muscular, curly haired, Spanish speaking Adonis.

"Hiiiii," I stuttered as my eyes briefly met his and then landed on his perfectly shaped bicep which I wanted to grab like a life jacket as I was drowning in instantaneous lust. Adonis took charge and placed my hands where they were supposed to go and we began to dance. I kept on stepping on his feet but he just laughed and swung me around to the music and then I laughed forgetting where I was.

Time flew by and then, it was time to go. Adonis said thank you, I said thank you and we both went our separate ways.

Chapter 10
Los Cabos Part One

When I got to the office on Monday, I felt depressed for so many reasons. I walked to my cubicle and passed Bob talking with Greg. I overheard that the client in San Antonio had not paid the first payment and that project would be halted. "Hey Sierra, can you come over here and join us when you put your stuff down?"

"Sure," I replied as I quickly put my purse down on my desk and turned back around to join them in the standing meeting.

"Our client in San Antonio has not paid us for our work so far and also, has not been responding to our emails for the last month. You need to stop doing your research and analysis on that project and switch gears to the Los Cabos project. You, me and Greg are going to Los Cabos next week to meet our client and you need to get prepared. That means coming in this weekend on Saturday and Sunday. We have a 7:00 am flight next Tuesday. Pack your sunscreen!"

Both Greg and Bob let out an almost coordinated laugh that had an aftertaste of inflated ego and false sense of pride. It was clear that Bob was grooming Greg and Greg was in it to win the highest prize he could. As just demonstrated, he had clearly trained himself to mirror Bob's actions and behaviors which he had probably learned from one of those self-help books on how to move up the corporate ladder.

A big time Spanish hospitality company somehow got in touch with Bob about doing a feasibility study for a proposed luxury project in Los Cabos. I had no idea where Los Cabos was but it sounded nice. I was tasked with having to write a portion of the report that dealt with shopping centers and malls in Los Cabos. But, there was not a lot of time to prepare anything except our suitcases. We ended up meeting on both Saturday and Sunday for a few hours to go over a tentative itinerary.

It was already Tuesday and I met Greg and Bob at the airport. In order to show team spirit, I sat next to Bob at the gate and I took a long look at what he was wearing: a blue denim button down shirt that began to be buttoned half way down his hairy chest, tucked into a pair of Wrangler blue jeans. This was a mismatched denim leisure suit at its finest complemented with a gold medallion necklace which made him look more like a drug smuggler from the 70's than a director at boutique consulting firm. Greg arrived just as the plane started boarding. He looked the part of some kind of a fashionable yuppie with a tight black, V-neck t-shirt that showed off his man boobs and was so small it stopped short of being tucked into his Levi's jeans waist thirty-six with a brown leather belt and black cowboy boots. I was trying to figure out if this is what they wore normally on a weekend or what they wore when it was a special occasion, like a work trip.

Grateful we were not sitting together, I was able to relax and I fell asleep during the flight. When I woke up, the plane had already landed. The three of us collected our bags and stepped out of the airport to wait for the car rental shuttle. It showed up and as we put our bags in the back of the van, the driver left the van to go into the airport. After about ten minutes sitting in the shuttle with no driver, Bob took matters into his own hands and drove the shuttle himself to the rental car office. No one seemed to notice that the van was being driven by someone else other than the rental car agency's employee. Bob sauntered up to the counter with the keys in hand explaining in Spanish that he had to wait. Greg translated that bit for me as we stood behind Bob silently trying to play along.

Bob turned around and said, "You two go sit down and I'll handle this." Both Greg and I followed the order to sit down and we watched the other customers who were mostly retired Americans with golf clubs.

The next thing I knew we were in our white, 4-door Kia Rio on the way to the hotel. I sat in painful silence, trying to figure out and anticipate what this trip would hold for me. I was looking forward to going to the beach and perhaps having some free time. I was surprised to see that all the hotels were like enclaves sitting on huge plots of beachfront land in which you needed a car to get from one place to another. The hotels were magnificent and the beach provided the backdrop for the most relaxing vistas. As Bob babbled on in his boss-smarter-than-thou-rhetoric, I was disappointed to learn that I wouldn't be able to go to swimming since the water was too rough and cold.

We pulled up to our hotel, which was a respectable level of upscale, and saw a few tour groups unload from their buses. I had been thinking that my room would just "happen" to be next to Bob or Greg. I wanted to tell the front desk agent that I was with one of the groups, but Bob and his putrid knockoff cologne lingered around me during check-in.

By some stroke of much deserved luck, my room was not located near Bob or Greg. And, I was also lucky that I had a great view of the water from my balcony. My first official business trip with an expense account could be a lot of fun, I thought to myself.

Chapter 11
Los Cabos Part Two

Towards the end of the trip with two days remaining we made a stop at Puerto Paradiso Shopping Mall. This was supposed to be a "fun" break, so Bob said as he directed Greg to stop there. The whole week, Greg was in charge of driving the Rio while Bob thoroughly enjoyed playing two roles: our boss and a back seat driver who never shut up. This trip was so grueling and traveling with Bob and Greg was wearing me down. Puerto Paradiso looked big enough for me to get some distance between the two of them.

Just as I was about to go my separate way, a tall attractive, well dressed, American retiree with a nametag that said Cheryl began talking to Bob.

"Welcome to Los Cabos. Would you like your next vacation to be free?"

"Well, young lady, yes I would." He had a sleazy look about him as he was warming up to get to know her better or at least get more information for our client.

"Oh, I haven't been called young lady in years. Where are you from, young man?" she said coyly.

I began to like Cheryl's style – serving bullshit back to bullshit – which was a bit bold considering she was supposed to be working in customer service and probably worked on commission for bookings.

"We're from Houston and we're here on business. This is my wife, Sierra, and business partner, Greg."

I had been distracted momentarily by a family of four wearing matching flip flops and who all were holding two gallon soda cups but as I heard the words "this is my wife, Sierra," I turned to look at Bob. He was looking straight ahead at Cheryl and ignoring me, his so-called wife.

I opened my mouth and started to say, "Who is your.."

But Bob totally ignored me and began to take over the last part of my question.

"Wow, we can go whale watching."

"Well, sir, I wanted to invite you and your wife to a presentation put on by Vacation Central, an agency here in Los Cabos that specializes in helping you find the best timeshare that matches your lifestyle perfectly."

Greg, in typical kiss-ass fashion, was taking notes. He was a true yes-man and dedicated to documenting everything. To a bystander, this looked like a normal situation with three people at a tourism kiosk. But on the inside, this was some dysfunction that kept on growing exponentially.

"OK, we'll see you both at 6:00 tonight and don't eat dinner. We'll have a buffet with make your own tacos. Do you like Mexican food?"

"Cheryl, I invented the taco. I wouldn't miss this buffet."

"Great. See you and the Mrs. tonight."

I did not like Cheryl anymore. Who would believe that I was this old fart's wife? I still didn't understand why the improvisation and the lies were necessary. It wasn't right.

The three of us walked back to the car in silence. Greg was looking at his phone. Bob was trying to find where Greg parked the Rio and I was like a deer caught in headlights barely able to keep up with them. At some point, I stopped walking and had to control myself from having an anxiety attack. What was going on here in this moment? I was having an out of body experience to try to escape this weirdness. I lost track of time and space looking up to the sky pretending I could fly back home to my bed in Houston.

"Sierra, honestly, what in God's name are you doing? Get in the car now," Bob barked from shotgun and I heard Greg start the car.

Like an obedient junior associate that I was, I got in and remained quiet.

"Now, Sierra, I don't want you to talk about this with anyone and I sure don't want you to blow this opportunity for our company. You have to pretend to be my wife so that we can go to this dinner tonight. Isn't this fun? We are going to be spies so that our client gives more money for future projects."

In my mind, I was saying, "Exploiting junior female coworkers into some crazy, concocted role-play situation on a business trip because you have a messed up family life back home...isn't this fun?" The logic behind me being betrothed to my boss for even a few painful hours to make more money for my employer made little to no sense in an age of equal rights for women. In a world where women continue to fight for equal pay for equal work, how does being blindsided with sexual harassment on a business trip advance women's role in society?

"Why can't Greg go with you? I mean he knows more about the client's needs since he has worked with them before."

"Are you kidding? Why would you think that we'd pretend to be homosexuals for this? It's more believable that you will be my wife."

This was out of some twilight zone Human Resources corporate training video. I wanted an attorney but not just any attorney. I wanted Gloria Allred to come right now to save me from this. I wanted to get on the next plane to D.C. and tell Obama how hard it is to be a young American, steeped in debt from college and grad school, trying to work to be a contributing member of society only to be met with an uphill battle as a junior professional. I never liked to play the "I'm a woman" card but this was something they didn't tell me about in graduate school. This was something my mother used to tell me stories about when she did work she couldn't wear pants to the office and how when she was a secretary some male executive asked her to spend the night with him after the holiday party. And now, it's my turn in a new generation that is more aware of sexual harassment but doesn't know how to handle it except blasting it on social media in an attempt to validate their pain.

Bob and Greg both laughed and then started talking about some guy in the office they thought was gay because he wore a pink tie once. This put me even more over the edge of the Equal Opportunity Employment Act being violated. I was trapped in the car. I couldn't jump out. I could give my two weeks' notice from the back seat. But somehow I didn't know what to say to stick up for my gay friends and to stick up for myself. I felt so angry I was getting sick to my stomach and just stared out the window the remainder of the car ride to the hotel.

We finally got to the hotel at 4:00 pm which left a little over an hour before we had to leave again to go to the taco buffet dinner. I got to my room and collapsed on the bed. Tears started to pour down my face. Raw anger, hurt, betrayal and fear continued to roll out of my soul and onto the printed duvet cover. My phone started to ring and I saw it was Bob. This call needed to go to voicemail. After about thirty more minutes my emotional explosion was almost over but it didn't solve my current predicament. What was I going to do tonight at the dinner as the fake Mrs. Bob? I grabbed my phone and listened to my messages. One was from Jennifer in San Francisco asking how Houston was going. I didn't even see that she had called because I was so wrapped up with this trip. We were long overdue for a chat post-JDate but I didn't have time to call her back now.

The second message was from Bob. He sounded strange in his voicemail: "Sierra, I need you to come to my room before we go. Have some things to prepare so we get what we need tonight."

Chapter 12
Los Cabos Part Three

My anger went further into overdrive as I tried to pull myself together in the bathroom. Here we go. Might as well call my Mom to see how she handled that situation in the story that she always managed to never quite finish. I wiped my running eye makeup with a washcloth and thought I was not going to reapply any makeup to look totally natural for this dinner. I saw in my cosmetic case my Swiss Army knife that I always packed when traveling. This trip being no exception, I got the idea to put the knife in my pocket for protection from whatever the rest of this day would bring. I felt as vulnerable as a mail order bride: stepping into a sordid unknown situation in a foreign country.

On the border of fight or flight, I took three deep breathes and walked to the other side of the hotel where Bob's room was. He had gotten the nepotistic suite since he knew someone's uncle who worked for the hotel company. I stood in front of the suite door a few minutes with my right hand turning over my knife in my pocket. Still remembering the day my Mom gave it to me as a going away present for my first trip to Brazil with Matteo. Matteo was a real man that protected and respected me during our year-long relationship and showed me that real men exist. While I never had to use the knife on that trip except to open wine, maybe now was the time to use it on someone. I wished Matteo was here now to help me. I wished someone was here to help me.

I got the courage to knock and heard Bob say "Just a minute." I took a step back and glanced over the terrace hallway that overlooked the parking lot. I heard the door unlock, but I did not move away from the edge of the terrace hallway. The door opened and I started screaming. I couldn't believe what was in front of my eyes. I was so disgusted and emotional that I couldn't stop screaming. Then, I yelled, "Put some clothes on."

Bob ignored what I said and instead came towards me in a too small towel wrapped below his eleven month pregnancy gut. He grabbed my shoulders and said, "Calm down."

I yelled louder, "I don't want to be your fucking wife you... fat... pervert of a boss!"

Out of nowhere, Greg showed up with a security guard. I cried out, "This is my boss and he is naked and he wants me to pretend to be his wife. Get your fucking hands off me."

Then, the security guard grabbed me in a bear hug type maneuver that helped me feel safely out of harm's way. "Is this true, sir?" asked the guard who was actually trying to help me.

"Of course not. She's my employee who has some emotional problems. She just needs to relax and have a shot of tequila."

Greg and Bob were the only ones laughing when the security guard gently let me go. He took out his note pad to start writing. The laughing stopped when Bob noticed that the security guard was writing an "Incident Report." Bob said, "Hold on, chief, no need for any of this. It's just a misunderstanding."

The security guard replied, "I'm required to document all incidents to our General Manager and the police, if necessary. Miss, please come with me. Sir, please put some clothes on."

I was two steps behind the security guard all the way down the terrace hallway to the elevators. When he stopped to turn left, my face landed in between his shoulder blades.

"Miss, are you OK? Don't worry, I'll help you."

He took my right shoulder and guided me towards the elevator in a type of herding maneuver that was firm but gentle. The elevator doors opened and with his hand still on my shoulder we both went in and he pressed L for lobby. He released my shoulder and said, "It's OK, Miss. We'll write this report up and talk to the General Manager about your boss's behavior."

Chapter 13
Los Cabos Part Four

We finally got to the front desk and then walked down a hallway I hadn't noticed before. There was a plain room with the sign "Security" over it. Inside, there was one table with four chairs and a phone on the wall. I had no idea what was going on but I felt like I was going to be interrogated like in CSI or another crime show I never watched because I got too scared.

"So, I will fill out this report and call the General Manager who will decide what to do. But I need you to tell me about your relationship with that man in the towel."

"His name is Bob, I mean, Roberto Martinez and he is my boss."

"OK, do you and your boss have a romantic relationship which may have flared up in the hallway?"

"Absolutely not. He wanted me to lie and pretend that we are married so that we could get information for our client who we are working for down here in Los Cabos."

"OK. OK. So, when he came out almost naked, did you feel threatened in any way?"

"Yes. I felt threatened and unsafe."

"That's all I need to know. The safety and security of our guests is very important to us. Give me one minute and I'll be back."

Without any other choice, I sat in the security room by myself with my arms crossed and my head resting on my forearms. In disbelief and in disgust, putting my head down was the only way I knew to try to get back some sort of sense of being grounded. My eyes were closed and the darkness began to soothe my frayed nerves. All of a sudden, I felt something on my head and I let out a shriek.

"Sierra, what is wrong with you? And, what did you tell them here?" Standing over me, like a huge Thanksgiving Day parade balloon, was Greg. He looked grotesquely enormous from my angle.

"Well, are you going to answer me?"

"I'm waiting to speak to the General Manager."

"You don't have to because Bob already spoke to him and took care of everything since his uncle knows some people. Unless you can beat the one thousand dollars he paid to settle it, I suggest you and I walk out of this room and we have dinner with Bob."

This was truly like a crime show and I hoped there were hidden cameras in this hotel security room. My brain was processing everything at warp speed while my mouth struggled to verbalize something intelligible. I got up and walked with Greg out of the room as I thought it was probably better just to follow along in this case.

"So you should go and apologize to Bob because he's waiting near the valet stand ready to go to dinner."

"OK, I'll do that after I go to my room."

With every intention not to do that, I went back to my room and didn't leave it until two hours later. I sat and watched Telemundo then went down to the lobby to get something to eat. The security guard saw me and came over.

"Hello, lady. Listen, are you OK?"

"Yes, I think so. Thank you for your help."

"You know, I'm not supposed to tell you this but they gave my boss some money so we can't do anything for you. But I'll watch out for you because you're a nice lady."

"Thanks."

It was confirmed then. Bob used his money and his connections to bribe someone to let this one go. At this time, I didn't know what to do or what to say. I went to the hotel restaurant and sat at the bar to enjoy some nachos and a Corona. It was the least the company could do after the events of today. As I was crunching down on the chips, I felt a bit of tension releasing. I was repeating the day's events over and over in my head. It was all too much. Who were these people I worked with? At least tomorrow, we were headed back to Houston and for some reason, there was a fortuitous miscommunication and I booked the

8:00 am flight instead of the 1:00 pm flight that Greg and Bob were on.

Chapter 14
Eye of the Tiger

My flight from Los Cabos arrived in Houston on Friday morning and I called Human Resources to schedule some time to talk about what had happened. Before we left for Los Cabos, Bob said we could take Friday off because we had to work long hours during the week. I was exhausted and went straight to my apartment from the airport and got confirmation that I would be speaking to someone in Human Resources at 3:00 pm.

Once I got home, I checked the mail. Then, I sat down and checked my bank balance. Friday was pay day and my bi-weekly paycheck had been directly deposited earlier in the day. I took this opportunity to make my October loan payment and check my balance owed.

The reality of my loan balance was depressing. After four payments, it barely decreased. And now returning from Los Cabos, I hated my job, boss and colleagues. I wondered if I could declare economic hardship to defer my loans if I quit this job. The situation with Bob at the hotel could mean me losing my job and putting my short-lived steady income into jeopardy. My third month was just starting so technically the first ninety days were not over yet. I guess I would go on a plan if my performance was not up to par but if I got let go, I wasn't sure if I'd get unemployment or not.

Instead of giving up, especially after the Los Cabos trip, I decided to go into financial planning mode and figure out how to save more money and spend less to maximize my current position while I still had it. I wondered if it was going to be possible to try to dedicate 10% of my monthly salary to eat, pay bills and make loan payments. After doing some more calculations, my phone started to ring. It was Bob. Seriously, why did Bob say we could have today off and then call me probably when he was getting off the plane? I did not answer this call and went back to try to figure out what was going to happen to my financial future.

This new financial model and budget had my heart beating a mile a minute. It seemed depressing, hopeless and dismal without end. Would people even want to hire me if after fourteen months of unemployment and three months of employment with a douche bag for a boss? I fell back on my bed. My eyes glued to the ceiling with numbers running in my head, flashbacks to Bob in a too small towel and Greg looking down at me in the hotel security office. Then, jolted out of the panic attack in the making, someone was knocking on my door which then put my adrenals into overdrive until I heard "Package for you, Sierra."

It was Wong, my mail carrier, who always had a smile on his face.

"Hi, Wong. How are you?"

I was really happy to see him in this moment.

"Living the dream"

"Good. Thanks for my package."

Here's a guy who told me he's second generation from China and loved America and the American Dream. He told me once he liked to work for the post office and deliver the mail to see how the real Americans live, not the ones you see on TV. I gathered even though he spoke English just fine he did have a Chinese accent. He didn't go to college; he didn't have loans.

I took the package and saw it was from my Mom. I was now anxious to open it and see what was inside forgetting about my current state of financial emergency. Opening the box, my eyes saw two plastic boxes of expired chocolate cupcakes from Costco, three Snickers bars and a bag of peanut M&M's. There was also a card at the bottom and I put it off to the side. Did my Mom think there was a sugar shortage in Houston? Or maybe I should have told her that I gained ten pounds in two months and that I couldn't fit into my pants anymore? What was I going to do with all this crap, especially the expired cupcakes? Taking it to the office was the best idea because at least they would eat it all and maybe they would get sick and maybe then they'd close the office because of some "foodborne illness" from Costco cupcakes that were recalled in Michigan but no one knew that in Texas.

Grabbing my phone to text my Mom a half-assed thanks, I saw Bob called twice and sent me a text message that said "All hands on deck meeting Sunday at 9:00 am at the office." Since when am I on call 24/7 for this company? This job was out of control. Bob was out of control. I was out of control. There was no choice except to see how long the contagion would last. There went my plans for taking a run early but not the plans for distributing the expired cupcakes.

After I read Bob's message, Human Resources called.

"Hi, can I please speak with Sierra?" said the voice of an older woman.

"This is she," I said standing up for the full effect of power.

"This is Marie from Human Resources and I wanted to talk to you about what you said you experienced on your business trip to Mexico. I'd like to hear your side of the story and let you know that what you tell me will remain confidential. We will decide how to proceed once we have your account of what happened."

"Hi, Marie. Well, on Thursday, Bob asked me to pretend to be his wife to go to a seminar for timeshares. He asked me to come to his hotel room before we went to the seminar. When I got to his hotel room, he answered the door in nothing but a towel wrapped around his waist. Hotel security came because I was terrified and started yelling."

"I see. Sierra, were you and Bob romantically involved on the trip?"

"No. I felt that this was pure sexual harassment and the hotel guard had written up an 'Incident Report' on the situation."

"OK, Sierra. Thank you for your time. That's all I needed from you. I'll be in touch if we decide we need your input again for this matter. Goodbye."

As I put my phone down after hanging up, I didn't know whose side Marie was on.

Chapter 15
Re-working

On Sunday, I arrived promptly at 9:00 am with all of my mother's cupcakes in addition to the M&M's in hand. Bob and Greg were ready in the conference room and Carla was setting up a projector.

"Mornin', Sierra," Carla said cheerfully with a smile.

"Good morning. Here are some goodies to get us through the day!"

"Thanks. Let's start," Bob said quietly staring at the cupcakes.

I was then stupefied to the point of speechlessness to see on the projector screen the report I finished in Los Cabos. But this version had "track changes" showing all the markups in red that someone had done to my report.

"This report is due to the client tomorrow and there's no way in hell we can present something like this after our trip. I'm not sure what happened but Greg can you tell us why you thought this was acceptable quality to receive from Sierra?"

Caught completely off guard, Greg opened his mouth but was also dumbstruck and unable to make any audible sound. He tried saying something but all that happened was that his face got brighter and brighter red just like the markups.

With all that took place in Los Cabos pending with Human Resources and now this impromptu meeting on a Sunday, I was about to put in my two weeks' notice. The emotional challenge of working in this type of environment had highlighted my inability to adapt successfully to this office culture. The only option I could think of was to save face and leave at least with some dignity intact. But, from Friday's calculation, I was so scared that I wouldn't have enough money and if I put in my two weeks' notice how would I ever get out of debt or go anywhere in life?

"Sierra, I need you to re-write this report today and give Greg each section when you finish it."

"Sounds good," I said as I bit into the stale, sugary shell of the dyed commercial icing. It hit the roof of the mouth and then the hydrogenated oil coating of the fake chocolate cake greeting my tongue. It was a good thing I had taken a bite of this, the grossest cupcake I'd ever tasted in my life, because it stopped me from saying the profanity that was on my mind.

"OK, let's finish this by today. You both can go back to your desks to work on it."

I took what was left of my cupcake back to my desk and unlocked my desk drawer. Then, I turned and saw Greg's head peaking over the cubicle.

"Hi, Greg."

"Sierra, cut this out. Start focusing on your job and not bringing in food or complaining to Human Resources.

"OK, Greg."

I turned slowly back to my computer and brought up version seven that had been displayed on the projector screen just a few minutes earlier. Not too bad, I thought, and then, I realized I had to bring up the comments and track changes. This was an issue that I had no idea how to come out on top. Taking out my file folder with my notes and research I tackled each comment and re-worked as best I could. The revisions kept me occupied until I realized I was hungry and thirsty. It was 1:00 pm and Bob and Greg were nowhere to be found. I sent Greg an email with my finished re-work. I only had three more sections to go and would do it after lunch.

Wondering if my go-to cheap lunch spot was open, I drove there to discover they are closed on weekends. I kept on driving around trying to find a place that was open when I just decided to go to Whole Foods. Grabbing a pre-packaged Caesar salad, I headed to the register and then ate in the parking lot before driving back to the office. It took me back to my days working at Whole Foods in D.C. It tasted the same as I remember and the dressing was so good that I used all of it on the salad.

But the cupcake, Caesar salad and the current high stress situation was not a good combination and led to digestive discomfort. I needed an antacid and decided to go to Walgreens before going back to the office.

By the time I got back to the office it was 2:15 pm and Bob and Greg were already in the conference room.

"Sierra, welcome back. Did you have a good three martini lunch?" Bob said snarkily.

"Just getting back from getting something for my stomach. I'm not feeling too well."

"Well, finish the report and then you can go home."

"OK."

All of a sudden, I was too tired and uncomfortable to say anything else. I sat back down at my desk and finished re-writing and adding more details to the last few sections of the report. The clock said 4:00 pm and I thought I was literally on the home stretch.

"All finished, Greg."

"We have to go to read it all again in the conference room."

With a heavy heart, head and stomach, I trudged back into the conference room. I was sure I had an ulcer developing right at this moment and displayed the Tums on the conference table where all would be able to see, not that they would care. Why did we have to go read it again and since we were supposed to be on billable time, wasn't all this re-work costing the client money? I did not understand this or the decisions about it all.

Greg connected his laptop to the projector and began to do another encore performance of the report. Reading the slides as if it was a soliloquy of corporate America, he was truly the understudy to Bob. By emulating Bob's pronunciation to almost perfection and even doing the short pause between slides Bob was famous for, Greg was giving an award winning and nauseating performance. It was all too much and my mind searched for something to distract itself from this kiss-ass-athon. As if it was divine intervention, a prayer came into my head that my sophomore theology class had to say every day. It was also the prayer for Alcoholics Anonymous and perhaps it served as a protective measure for those situations where heavy alcohol use was thought the only way to get through.

Lord, grant me the serenity to accept the things I cannot change. The courage to change the things I can and the wisdom to know the difference.

The serenity, courage and wisdom were all escaping me at the moment as I thought it was better for me to zone out to protect myself from something I obviously had a hard time accepting. In this state of eating Tums like popcorn and praying in a conference room with a projector and screen, I got through all the "edits" which took until 9:00 pm. And, when I finally got home I checked my phone to see a text from

Pamela: "See you tomorrow in office at 8:30 ☺." The smiley face was a passive aggressive way to somehow offer a happy ending to the message and perhaps, also the insanity that the job had become for me.

From left to right, I felt like I had been blindsided. First, with the actual work and now, with the politics of so many things I could not even being to comprehend. I had a list of questions I was going to bring to the meeting at 8:30 am. I had to prepare to power-through tomorrow and I needed to wear something nice, preferably clean, too. Since I was supposed to do laundry today but had to go to the marathon meeting instead, I would see in the morning what I had clean or almost clean. I just needed to close my eyes and take a rest.

Chapter 16
A Compromise

My alarm rang at 6:30 am and snooze was the best option. Although I could not really snooze as I would have liked because my head was racing with all the scenarios of what could happen today. Maybe I'll get a promotion because after all I wrote most of the report and Pamela was happy with me so she put that smiley in the text message. Or maybe I'll get transferred to another team because Greg realized I'm really smarter than him. I knew I had to put on my positive, can-do attitude, take a shower and find something to wear.

Standing in the bathroom waiting for hot water, I smiled in the mirror and kept on smiling until the smile turned into grinding my teeth. It was only until the mirror started to steam up that I knew I had to get in the shower and get clean. When the water hit the crown of my head, I began to cry because I knew today was going to suck, no matter how much I smiled, no matter how nice I looked, no matter how fake I was.

The shower was a much needed, emotional escape. I finished with a cold rinse that I had read somewhere was great for your emotions and your circulation. After the shower, I got dressed in the same suit I interviewed in as it was still clean and thought it was symbolic to wear a suit to the beginning and the end of whatever was coming my way. Although, I had to wear my bikini bottoms since I was out of clean underwear.

It was now 8:00 am and I had exactly ten minutes to dry my hair and put on my makeup. By 8:15 am, I was out the door with the heat up full blast to try to finish drying my hair in the car. I strolled into the office at exactly 8:28 am and went straight to Pamela's office. The office was strangely quiet for a moment with Greg's and Bob's desks untouched and their boisterous voices noticeably absent.

Pamela's office light was on and I went to the door and did a polite knock with one knuckle. But Pamela was not in the office. Her coat was on the chair and her computer was on. I noticed she had some files on her desk and an interoffice envelope.

I decided to walk back to my desk to put my bag down. I was about to sit, when I saw Pamela come out of the conference room.

"Hi, Sierra. You want to join us in the conference room, please?"

"Sure," was my answer to the question that wasn't really a question. I walked slowly into the conference room to see sitting on the right side of the table Bob and Bob's boss who I only met during the interview process. I remembered him because of the sheer size of his morbidly obese body. Neither he nor Bob stood up to greet me as I entered the room. Pamela took the seat at the head of the table.

"Sierra, why don't you sit here on my left?" said Pamela motioning with her left hand to the seat closest to her.

"Now Sierra, this will be brief. We wanted to talk to you about a few things and see if we couldn't work something out. As you told me before, you've been unsure about what you want to do and it certainly shows through your work quality. Also, your behavior is jeopardizing yourself and your career, namely by filing a false sexual harassment claim with Human Resources. We spoke to Marie about what you said and set the record straight. Now, let's just forget those little things and focus on the future."

"Sierra, you should know your sexual harassment claim has been dismissed by Human Resources for lack of supporting evidence," interjected Bob.

"I didn't hear back from Marie about that and don't think this is right."

"That's why we're telling you now," Bob said with a slight tilt of the head that made him look like a bulldog that is trying to figure out what just happened to his toy.

"We wanted to talk to you about next steps that will be better for you, Sierra," said Pamela.

"Sorry, next steps for what?" I said taking both hands and adjusting my suit jacket to show I was in control of me, if nothing else.

"We're going to offer you a transfer to a new team in San Francisco or a package to be let go today."

"OK, I think I understand what's going on. Transfer to California? What type of job would I be doing on that new team there?"

"You'll be an analyst at the same salary level and have a fresh start with the company, but we can't really guarantee much more. We realize maybe we shouldn't have asked you to do certain things here in Houston. San Francisco would give you a new opportunity to begin again. The past few months have shown us you are a good employee but had quite a few challenges in the Houston office."

"Sierra, what do you want to do? Time is money. We need an answer now to expedite this process," Pamela said looking at me with the same expression she had when she dismissed the first taco salad with sour cream.

"With all due respect, I can't afford to be out of a job with all my loans. But, I want all of you to know I tried my best and did everything that was asked of me. I have finished my work assignments and met all of my deadlines. Thank you for the offer to transfer to San Francisco. I'll take that option."

"Good. Looks like everyone wins," Bob said smiling while looking at his boss, then Pamela, then me.

"Sierra, meet me in my office now to sign the paperwork and we'll set a date for you to start in two weeks in the San Francisco office," Pamela said as she went towards the door of the conference room.

Pamela opened the door for me to exit and then quickly closed the door. I stood there standing outside the door and heard, "Bob, you need to hire another Latino for your team and this time not another woman. If we don't meet our diversity numbers, we won't be able to get our office remodeled."

Chapter 17
Moving On

It was decided for me that I would be starting my new job in San Francisco in exactly two weeks. I would have the next week to wrap up my projects in the Houston office and have a few introductory meetings over the phone with the San Francisco team. I also had to pack my apartment and my desk. The company was paying for my plane ticket there but there was no relocation bonus this time.

My exit interview for the Houston office was scheduled later that week. I was in the process of packing my apartment up piece by piece. I didn't really know what to expect and I would go through phases of depression and elation. The little voice in my head kept on urging me to look for back-up jobs just in case the team in San Francisco was the same or worse than the Houston team because of that whole "company culture" thing people talk about. I thought I should call home to tell my parents what was going on.

"Hi, Mom. How are you?"

"Hi, Sierra. So good to hear your voice! I just got back from shopping! And, I got the most amazing cashmere sweater twin set and I was thinking this is probably something you would need, too, for your job, although I don't know what the weather is like in Houston during the fall."

"Well, I'm not going to find out. I got a transfer to the San Francisco office and will be moving there next week," I said in a monotone way.

"What happened? Oh, before I forget, did Lexie tell you about her Mario? He came over for dinner last week and what a catch he is! Lexie and Mario – they are sooo cute," she swooned

"Uh, no, haven't talked to Lexie in a while. A lot has happened that I haven't told you guys about. I just hope that San Francisco is a better place for me," I sighed into the phone.

"Sierra, you can't afford to be without a job. Everyone knows that. Is your friend Jennifer still there? That might be good for you since you don't have a boyfriend," she said.

"Yes, that's what I was thinking, too. I'm looking forward to seeing her and having a fresh start. I'm shipping my things and then I fly out next week. I gotta go, Mom. I'll call you when I make it to San Francisco," I said quickly to avert any possible further discussion.

"Bye, Sierra. Call me if you need anything and be safe," she said.

I had to get going to make it to my therapy session. Since I couldn't really talk about my emotions with my Mom and I hadn't made many friends in Houston, I found a psychotherapist I named Dr. Mean, after my first visit. Dr. Mean was a typical Texan: very tall, dyed blonde hair, and a twang. I didn't care who the therapist was I just needed someone to listen or pretend to listen. The good thing was that she was covered by insurance and had an office close by.

My first visit with Dr. Mean was filled with no-nonsense, direct questions about why I was there. I took the seriousness to mean that this was real therapy and I should expect results. Translating her coldness into being mean, I thought maybe that's what I needed. I scheduled today's follow-up visit with her to help me prepare for another transition to a new city. I ended up wanting to talk but just kept on crying. Dr. Mean told me to stop crying and instead of crying I should read inspirational books and even said I should listen to "I Will Survive." I felt so awful sitting there staring at her brown roots and then I began to have empathy for her. There was silence after some time and then she said, "You are just an ugly duckling, waiting for swans."

No, actually I was waiting for my start date in San Francisco. Ugly or not, duckling or swan, Texan or not, my last desire was to be treated fairly and professionally. Dr. Mean's condescending tone in calling me an ugly duckling stung like a jellyfish and throbbed in my soul as I got up to leave without paying her. It hurt to be superficially judged on the basis of how I looked by Pamela and now Dr. Mean.

From what I read online, therapy can be an individual journey, filled with opportunities for personal growth but comes down to the relationship between the therapist and patient. I didn't discount the two sessions I had with Dr. Mean. If anything, the timing was right to call me out on not fitting in and challenging me to do better in the upcoming transition. One thing I knew after spending three months in Houston, I needed to focus on presenting myself better and focus more on relationships that were healthier for me.

The same week as my second appointment with Dr. Mean brought my five second, Houston office exit interview with Marie. She had asked what I liked best about the Houston office and if there was anything I would change. I said I liked that there was always parking available and I would change the culture to be more supportive of women. I also said it would be better if we were able to pick our own mentors. And, with that, I was thanked for my input and wished well on my new job in San Francisco.

Chapter 18
Your Junk Is Your Junk

The boxes that helped get me to Houston three months ago now were going to help me get to San Francisco. The moving company in D.C. had provided everything – bubble wrap, packing tape, and strong reusable moving boxes – all of which I saved. This was the last weekend I would be in Houston and I had to get packing.

I stared at the empty boxes feeling as empty as they were. The events of the last two weeks caused me to question how I was living. After some time, I looked at my stuff. Some of it wasn't even mine but hand-me-downs from alleged generous family members who had "given" to me what they had no longer needed. A good part of my life was always trying to make do with less. From my college days to now, I could say "no" to these castoffs but I seemed to always be in financial need. So the mismatched pots, orphan plates, my grandmother's real silver silverware were part of my default bohemian, continuously frugal style until I guess I got married and then got to pick out registry items that matched. Then, the same relatives who gave me the stuff they didn't want would have to spend money on stuff that I did want.

As I put some of this stuff into boxes, I thought these antiques kept me closer to my family from to time to time. At other times, especially when

I drove by Kirk's antique junk yard, I felt my things from family members needed to go there. And, now packing these things I didn't really want, the idea revisited me to dump this stuff at Kirk's for it might feel incredibly freeing to confront my angst about Houston, working and my family by getting rid of some stuff.

While it was not a good day to be outside, it was the right time for me to purge all the emotional junk that I could. I carried two boxes of stuff out to my car, got in and started driving to Kirk's. I pulled in the driveway behind the famous truck with the painted side sign that said "Your Junk, Our Treasure" which made the selling of a lifetime of accumulation so banal. It could have been easily reversed so that it read "Your Treasure, Our Junk" as anyone could tell by the small grassy excuse of a yard. I parked and stared out of passenger's window at the junk getting soaked in the downpour.

In the yard, the landscape of odds and ends at Kirk's was especially assaulting to anyone who likes order. Two three-drawer beige file cabinets, one oak-looking dining room table, one mossy green reclining lawn chair, and a white wicker couch were visible. The lawn ornaments were as famous as Kirk's slogan and there were always a couple of pink flamingos, trolls and Mary statues that found themselves in between the file cabinets and assorted furniture. The house that was also a showroom of sorts was dark with no lights even though the "Yes, Were Open" sign said otherwise.

Someone's material possessions and perhaps their own lifestyle similar to mine were on always on display. Maybe the previous owners of the crap that ended up at Kirk's also experienced the depressing, soul-crushing reality of hand-me downs, loan payments and other people's false righteousness of paying it forward. Whatever the trolls' and other objects' backstories were, it didn't really matter to Kirk. It was all business.

As I took some of the boxes out of the car that were supposed to go to San Francisco with me, the rain kept coming. Standing there getting soaked with a box in my arms, I thought: if this is life, if life comes to this, a yard full of shit accumulated over a lifetime that no one wants, that gets soaked because not even Kirk cared enough to take care of the stuff he's trying to sell, then here's my shit that I never bought and I can't afford to buy for myself anyway. The rage that was rising up about my job and about everyone exploded as I chucked the box in the direction of the house. The box landed two feet in front of me and broke open. The now broken orphan plates finally found a home where they belonged.

Lighter and with a renewed sense of purpose, I drove home and finished packing what was left. The remaining six boxes that were going to go to San Francisco were taken to UPS to be shipped with insurance the cheapest and fastest way possible. I used Jennifer's address for the six boxes and packed my clothes in my two suitcases. I was as ready as I would ever be to get on the plane and say goodbye to Houston.

Chapter 19
Welcome to San Francisco

The much anticipated departure from Houston happened on a Thursday. I checked my two bags and then boarded the plane to San Francisco. Taking a moment to realize that the last time I was at this airport I was coming from Los Cabos in a much different state. Today, the sense of relief to leave that situation and Houston behind forever was like nothing like I'd ever felt before making me lighter, happier and confident. I was alive and looked forward to my new, West Coast life.

As the plane took off, I watched Houston disappeared from my window seat. Goodbye, Houston. Goodbye, Texas. I could finally relax knowing that I had a new job and new apartment waiting for me in some funny named part of San Francisco called the Tenderloin.

I started looking for my new San Francisco apartment the day I signed the office transfer document in Pamela's office. I thought it would be easy because San Francisco was a major city. But, searching for a place online before I got to San Francisco was a nightmare. Prices seemed extraordinarily high and I wasn't sure if these prices were real or if it would be some type of scam where someone in Nigeria would want me to send my deposit for one month's rent. In addition, Jennifer was too busy to help me and there was no way I could stay with her and her two roommates because her place was way too small, she said. But, I could store some boxes there.

My post-Houston real adult life started when I took a cab from San Francisco International Airport to my new home in the Tenderloin. My sight unseen apartment in this neighborhood was one that touted itself on the website as a lower priced alternative to corporate housing and ideal for students. It turned out to be a renovated one star hotel from the 1980's that had a mini-fridge and microwave in each room. My room had two full beds just for me with faded palm tree bedspreads, a bathroom with a decent bathtub, fresh towels and a cracked window that faced a fire escape from the adjacent building. The lobby level had an extended back area past the front desk that included what was once a restaurant but now was a shared kitchen and had a long communal table. There was also a pool table and a TV off to the left.

With this new apartment, at double the price of what I was paying in Houston, I did some new budget spreadsheets to figure out how I would actually live. The good thing about Houston was that things were relatively cheap and there was no state income tax in Texas. I had paid off enough on my credit card to afford my deposit and one month of rent at $1600/month at this place and it was clear that I had to guard the remaining balance I did have so I did not overextend my credit. Now, I would have to think of new ideas to make this move work economically and re-start my frugal ways.

But Jennifer had told me there are so many more jobs in the San Francisco Bay Area and that it was the land of "milk and honey" with the most resident millionaires in the US that live there. Jobs complete with incredible benefits and high pay aka golden handcuffs at internet companies keep young people happy in long-term cushy jobs, even though some people have tech necks and hunchbacks as a result. And, some companies even let you telecommute all the time. It'd be easy to get a job like this because companies would want to hire an MBA, she had said. It was a good time to be here with many, educated young people starting their own companies and living the American Dream. It wasn't at all like Detroit or the East Coast where jobs were hard to find and people were depressed. Everyone liked to go outside and hike and on Monday talk about their weekend and add, "We're so spoiled."

I called Jennifer about two hours after I got to my new apartment but she did not answer so I ventured out to find something to eat. As I left the building I wasn't sure if I should take a left or a right on Market Street. A group of Korean tourists were walking to the left and thought I would casually follow them to see where they were going.

While they all had their phones out and selfie sticks, they were not taking any pictures or looking around at the stores and restaurants. They all were very close to each other and walking at a fast pace. I switched my focus from their group to the surroundings and saw some men standing near a store that had the biggest subwoofers I'd ever seen. I accidentally made eye contact with one guy and then he said, "Weed. Weed. Weed."

I was startled and jumped a little and then started walking faster to try to keep up with the group again. Soon I realized that it wasn't uncommon to run into those selling a wide variety of herbs as about two minutes after I saw the first group of men, I saw another group of whom I did not make eye contact.

By this point, I had only seen an audio store, a dollar store and a sunglass store. I wondered why there weren't any police arresting these guys for selling drugs on the street. I also wondered how long I had to walk to find something to eat. I finally saw a taqueria next to a diner. The taqueria seemed like the better option as I was sure I could get a bean burrito for a couple bucks. Upon entering the taqueria, I was confused to see that the cash register and small kitchen behind it were walled off by plexi-glass that looked like it hadn't been clean since it was installed. I didn't really care to try to analyze what purpose the plexi-glass was supposed to serve because I was hungry and ordered my bean burrito to go.

After I got the bean burrito, I headed back on the opposite side of the street to avoid the independent business men. A woman at a bus stop caught my eye because she was wearing tight blue spandex pants revealing every dimple of cellulite she had along with socks and Crocs. I reached down to touch my cellulite to reassure myself I was the only one that knew it existed under my jeans. I noticed that this woman had some chicken wings in a small, brown waxed cardboard box in her palm and was balancing a half-eaten one between her forefinger and thumb.

"San Francisco is the nastiest city. One of these mother fuckin' hobo pricks be shittin' on the seat. No damn dog did it. 'Em one of these bastards. If it weren't for the money, I'd be back there with you," said the woman into her phone that was cradled between her neck and shoulder.

At least she had someone to talk to which was more than I could say of my bean burrito.

Chapter 20
A Quiet Storm

The whole weekend I spent decompressing in bed and watching TV. Monday morning came fast and I walked to the new office which was near the famous landmark TransAmerica building. It had a more upscale feel than the Houston office. The office was on the 15th floor allowing natural light into the office and had blue and green for the color scheme. This was in sharp contrast to the 1980's style, gray tinted windows in the Houston office. Also, the cubicles in the Houston office were non-existent here in the open structure with a few glass wall offices on the periphery. The secretary asked me to sit on the stiff gray, designer wool sofa, while she let my new manager, Steve, know I was here.

I noticed the magazines on the office coffee table included issues of *Time*, *Modern Luxury* and *Forbes* and wondered if anyone read those. I decided just to stare at them as I was trying to come up with intelligent questions to ask about my new job. Last week's initial phone calls were superficial in nature and were more like another round of interviews. I was introduced in the first call to Steve, who's intranet profile was similar to Bob's although Steve was about ten years younger than Bob and had more experience with luxury apartment projects. Steve moved from New York to San Francisco almost one year ago to build the West Coast practice. From his picture, he looked like the typical executive: light brown hair with a conservative cut parted to the right, blue eyes, white shirt, dark blue jacket and a dark green tie.

"Hi, Sierra. Steve. Nice to meet you." Steve appeared from around the corner and extended his arm to shake my hand. In person, he was tall and fit, and again well dressed with a dark suit and tie.

"Hi, Steve. Sierra. Thanks for this opportunity," I said, giving a firm handshake that was a little too firm as I rolled his pinky knuckle by accident.

"Please follow me."

Following Steve to the to the glass-walled conference room next to the lobby, I saw no one else in the office. We entered the conference room and there was a folder waiting on the table which made choosing a seat easy. I took the seat with the folder and Steve sat opposite me.

"Thanks for coming in today. We're happy to have another person on our team. Just to let you know we are waiting on a few deals in the pipeline and don't have a lot of work for you right now. So, we prepared the folder there for you to get started learning more about what we do here in the San Francisco office."

"Thanks. How is the San Francisco office different from the Houston office?"

"We're all a part of the same company and to be honest, I'm not entirely sure what the Houston office focused on – projects in Mexico maybe? Here in San Francisco, we are doing more luxury apartment projects now. How much do you know about San Francisco?"

"It's my first time here and I'm learning everything I can."

"Good. Well, read those materials over the next few days and we'll get you set up for access to our share drives and other documents we use here. Welcome aboard."

"Thanks. Looking forward to being on your team, Steve."

Steve abruptly left the conference room and the receptionist appeared, "Hi Sierra, I'll show you to your new desk."

My new desk was a seat at a six person table. Each place had a large monitor and a file cabinet underneath. No one else was seated at the table and I was unsure if anyone had ever sat there. As I sat down, I noticed that the file cabinet still had plastic on it.

"Nice and new I see!"

"Your combination for the file cabinet is here with the Wi-Fi password. Any other questions just let me know.

"Thank you. I'm sorry I didn't get your name."

"Oh, it's Nora. You're welcome."

"Thanks, Nora."

I sat down and opened the binder that Steve gave to me. It was standard corporate marketing one-pagers about the company and the San Francisco practice. There was a case study of a real estate developer in San Francisco that hired the firm to conduct a feasibility study for a luxury high rise project in the Tenderloin that was not too far away from my place. I wondered what rent was like there and maybe all those millionaires that Jennifer told me about really did live there.

After I finished reading that, I turned on my computer and checked my email. Nothing. I thought it might be a good idea to look up that real estate project close to me to find out more details about it. It was a two year old project that involved some Chinese investors who worked with a real estate development company to construct the 88-unit luxury building. I had no idea how I would work on these types of projects or what would be my role.

Steve came up from behind and said, "Hi, Sierra. I'm going to be sending you a list of properties to research and add the appropriate information that we need. You can work from home the next few days and we'll see you on Friday with it completed ready to give me a summary of what you found."

"OK, Steve. Sounds good."

"I have to go now to another appointment. See you Friday," he said quickly as he walked out of the office towards the elevators.

Chapter 21
The Tenderest of Loin

After Steve left, I worked for a while on the spreadsheet and then I left around 5:00 pm. I took my computer and began walking back to the Tenderloin. Saving money needed to be a priority and I knew I had to make little steps like walking instead of public transport. But, my computer bag got to be heavy about half way home and I needed to stop somewhere. My body already made the decision as my feet were walking into a café almost on their own and grabbed a table first before ordering.

"You mind if I sit here?"

"No, don't mind at all," I replied politely with a smile. I was pleasantly surprised that this guy, who was a respectable level of clean cut cuteness, wanted to sit and talk to me.

"Thanks. How's your day going?" he asked.

"Not bad. And you?" I said while smiling and thought this is amazing. A cute guy is talking to me now.

"I'm working on my startup that helps people like us find affordable housing," he pitched me.

"Oh, great. I could use that since I just moved to San Francisco and my crappy apartment is in the Tenderloin," I said casually, not sure if he was trying to impress me or something else was going on that I didn't understand.

"Yeah, we only charge a monthly subscription of fifty bucks for a daily listing of all properties within a twenty-mile radius of San Francisco. And, we'll even print you pay stubs if you need to show proof of a job for your application. Here's my card. See you around."

"Bye," I said as I took his card and watched him walk away. I thought maybe he was interested in more than just telling me about his startup and really wanted to buy me a coffee and ask me out. But, I just got to San Francisco and didn't really know what guys were about here. What's worse is that I could use his company's services, if it was legit. But for that price of a glorified curated Craigslist listing email, I thought I could save my money for something better and find a guy who actually asks me out in a way I understand.

I looked around the café and saw many young, fit people who almost all had MacBooks or iPhones out. No one was overweight here. And, instead of blonde highlights like I saw so much of in Houston, some had green or blue accents on their ends. They all seemed to be very dressed down in t-shirts and hoodies with a couple of guys wearing plaid shirts. But it was a bit strange as no one was talking as if the customers really did want to listen to the alternative chill music being piped in.

After I rested a moment without buying anything at the café, I walked back to my true shithole of a home. While my time in Houston was short, that apartment with the pool was infinitely better than my current living situation. I already knew I didn't want to live here and kept on reminding myself it was just temporary until things settle down. In all honesty, this apartment was one of the most degrading places I had ever lived in my life. Worse than a basement in D.C. A PO Box would need to be in order if I was to live here because if anyone found out that I did live here, I'd be judged, discriminated against and pitied.

The old hotel was really a SRO, a single room occupancy apartment building. This information wasn't disclosed on the website but I learned this from a sign in the lobby. My building and other buildings like this have low priced units typically with a shared bathroom or shared kitchen. When I was looking for places, I came across some listings for residential hotels and some of these hotels were SRO's. I really had no idea what a SRO was, but I knew I could not afford to rent a normal studio in San Francisco.

The living environment is much like a college dormitory with a few notable exceptions. The first exception is not everyone went to college in a SRO and the diversity of inhabitants that I've seen so far in my building has been disorienting. Single people, couples and young families from different parts of the country and the world were all were living at my

SRO. Most of single people were more transient like me and came to work, study English or have an extended vacation. The couples that I met were a mix of those who had been living there for quite some time and others who were doing what the single people were doing. The families were mostly non-native English speaking families and not sure what they were doing but having four people in a converted hotel room didn't sound like fun since I could hear a good deal through the thin walls.

The second exception is that there are no quiet hours. So, this means, my neighbor with what I diagnosed as Tourette's can bang his head against the wall as many times as he wants at 2:00 am and the family on the other side can sing lullabies in a foreign language over kids crying. This is why I hadn't talked to my neighbors or anyone else that lived in the building. The third exception is that security consists of a narcoleptic guard who is supposed to keep the residents safe. I'm not sure why this guard even exists if the good majority of time he is asleep in his chair not watching the security cameras or checking IDs.

These exceptions may be why the rent is discounted below market rate and why these building serve as affordable housing. It was strange to me that Steve had asked me to find out where all the SRO's were located in San Francisco as part of the research I was doing for him. Since I now had firsthand experience with SRO's, I could find out more easily than before. The front desk where the guard was had a list of current SRO's and I could just borrow that, I thought. But, I would have to make sure that I didn't divulge any detail that would make it obvious that I actually lived in one. If Steve found out that the new MBA hire who just transferred from Houston lived in a SRO located in the Tenderloin that would be extremely embarrassing. What would be more embarrassing than that is if I got evicted so that the same Chinese investor client would buy my SRO thanks to my research so he could tear it down to build another luxury condo building.

Chapter 22
Passionless

After three weeks in the San Francisco office, I had little to show for it, except a lot of research on SRO's. I had gone to a couple of Meetups to try meet new friends and potential dates. I gave my number to a few people to go have a drink but no one called or followed up on going out. Maybe I was too passive because internally I was still trying to figure out what happened in Houston. Again, my social life was on the back burner as I knew I had to focus on this new job until I was a little more established in San Francisco. I still hadn't seen Jennifer and only got a few texts from her which had been disappointing.

Steve only came into the office on Fridays and usually would email me once or twice a week some topics to research and present to him when he was in. I thought this seemed odd and I wasn't sure how he viewed my research as he never really said much after I presented my work.

It was end of the fourth week and I was in Steve's office going over the latest Excel spreadsheet of names of buildings. When I finished, he looked up at me and asked, "Sierra, are you happy here?"

"Yes, I'm enjoying doing this research for you and want to do more projects."

"That's not what I meant. I meant do you have passion for Brown and White and your work?"

"I sure do."

"Look, let me just cut to the chase. We wanted to give you a second chance and to be honest, I don't have enough work for you to do here. I had some more ideas of how we can work together but I'm not seeing a strong sense of initiative on your part. I also have no idea what motivates you or what your passion is. Based on what I heard you did in Houston and what you're doing now in San Francisco, we're going to have to let you go. You can pack up your things now and Human Resources will be in touch. I wish you the best, Sierra."

"OK. Thanks for the second chance."

I walked back to my soon to be former desk, gathered my stuff and started to leave when Nora called out, "We need your badge before you leave," as if she knew all along that today was going to be my last day.

Taking my badge holder off of my cardigan, I threw it towards Nora's desk. I took the stairs down to the first floor and went out the door. It was the start of rush hour and I was amidst the mass exodus from all the nearby offices. I stood for another few moments, close to the side of a building to avoid being trampled by this crowd. I was dazed and thinking about these nameless people and wondering what their passion was. Just this morning, I was one of them, but now looking at them from the outside, I wondered why there is such a push for working for your passion when the majority of people here have a strong determination for leaving the office.

The notion of doing and being fully devoted to one's passion has always confused me and, now, standing outside speechless and jobless, I lost myself. What was I supposed to be like in the office to show or fake this passion Steve wanted to see? Will there ever be something that will keep me like a hamster on a wheel working hard to get out of debt so I could be passionate about life?

Keeping the status quo of perceived passion is what I didn't know how to do. The mantra "follow your passion" has become lip service for employers and a default for people that have a passion to please other people. Because everything is so much more acceptable when someone says they want to follow their passion at work. Some people are passionate for things that don't translate into money and are not job related. Other people like me didn't know what they were passion about or if they will ever be passionate enough to please other people.

In another moment of self-reflection, still blankly staring at the masses I thought "Here I am. Just got fired after four months of working at my first real job post-business school that took me fourteen months to get. I live in San Francisco and my apartment building is half purgatory, half DMV where no one knows how they got there or how long they'll be there."

"Oh sorry, I didn't see you there," said a guy on a scooter as he brushed by me. I was still standing outside my now former building unable to move. So fast was that encounter to jolt me out of my self-pity, anti-passion monologue that I barely noticed he was wearing a bright yellow jacket with RestEZ on it. That's an interesting name for a company and one heinous jacket.

Chapter 23
Making Do

Within a few days after getting let go, I accepted my current situation, took responsibility for myself and applied for unemployment. The process to file for unemployment went smoothly and within two weeks I started receiving checks on a regular basis. I could keep the unemployment until I found a new job and had to report regularly on what jobs I was applying for.

Since I had so much free time, I wanted badly to meet some friends and go out once and a while. I was disappointed that I still hadn't been able to get together with Jennifer and bummed out I really wasn't meeting anyone new who actually made plans to go out to lunch or to a bar. Everything seemed so transitory and noncommittal here. A night like tonight made me want to go out with friends instead of try to cook something in a communal kitchen. But I did not have any friends and I did not want to go out alone and spend money.

Walking down to the communal kitchen, I saw some young people getting ready to go out. I sighed then looked away still smelling their perfume and cologne as I entered the kitchen. I opened the fridge and realized I didn't have anything left to eat. This was now a food emergency. The executive decision to use some of the reserved unemployment check for a trip to Trader Joe's was quickly ratified by my growling stomach.

"Hey honey, close the fridge!" I heard a voice say from behind.

"Yeah, I was just checking to see what I had left in here," I said as I closed the door.

"You want some of my Spam? I'm making my specialty – a fried Spam sandwich," the voice said. I turned around to see an elegant, elderly woman holding a can of Spam and smiling at me.

"Oh, that's nice but I will go out to get something."

"What's your name, honey?"

"It's Sierra. And, you?"

"I'm Bev. Bev from Brooklyn they call me. I've been here twenty years, probably before you were born."

"Nice to meet you, Bev. Would you like to get a coffee one day? I've got some free time and we could go to the new place across the street."

"Sure, honey. You know, you look like you're worried. Remember: If it doesn't kill you, then it doesn't kill you. I'm in room 604. Come by and we'll grab a coffee." And with that she went to take out a frying pan to make her Spam specialty and I left the kitchen to head out the front door.

Walking to Trader Joe's, I asked myself how a nice lady like Bev could look that good by eating Spam and living there for twenty years? Then, I thought about my situation and the people I now saw on the streets. How long could I go on with my unemployment checks, living in my SRO, seeing people on the street who are or perhaps were in a similar situation to myself? Why is there such a huge disparity in San Francisco between the affluent and the poor?

These questions also coupled with the frantic anxiety of my financial situation disconnected me from my body until I felt my shoe sink into something slowly. I looked down and saw it was a pile of someone's vomit. I then vomited. The anxiety, the filth, the fact that someone's vomit was now on my shoe, all added up to two piles of vomit on the sidewalk.

I grabbed a Kleenex from my bag and wiped my mouth and kept walking. I was almost there and I couldn't stop to clean the vomit off my shoe for fear that something might happened to me in this area. While there were a few crazy people milling around that saw or maybe they didn't see my performance, everything was fine and no one said anything to me as I put a determined face and continued my journey to Trader Joe's.

The bright lights of Trader Joe's were a welcome relief. I looked at myself in the reflection of my cellphone to make sure I looked somewhat presentable to enter. I was ok. I was alive. I just looked pretty bad.

After the automatic doors opened, I made a beeline for the bathroom. It's one of the perks I enjoy at Trader Joes – a nice bathroom. Wow, I really looked awful. I have to go back to the gym. I have to get a haircut. I need a facial… This list went on and on until I heard a knock at the door. I need to leave this restroom.

I exited the restroom, more calm and collected. I grabbed a free coffee sample with soy creamer and helped myself to the lukewarm turkey gravy and stuffing sample. Now, I was feeling better. I made my way around the store and picked up just a few essentials, to save time as it was getting late.

"Good evening, miss. Did you find everything you were looking for?" the 40-something year old cashier with Vince on his name tag said in a monotone way.

"Yes. Thanks, Vince." I quickly replied to speed the checkout process up.

"I'll need to see your ID."

"Oh, it's always a compliment. Here you go. And, I'll just put this stuff in my purse here."

He looked at my ID and then back at me. "I think you are old enough to buy a real purse," he snapped, as he put my items into my black bag I called a purse. Really, it was a small free reusable bag that was given to me after I made a purchase somewhere I don't even remember.

"I can't afford the purse I really want," I responded a bit defensively and caught off guard that the cashier at Trader Joe's would care what kind of purse I had.

To which he replied, "What do you want...a Vuitton?"

"I need a job before I can afford anything."

I went from vomiting, to buying a few essentials, to being judged by the cashier at Trader Joe's. My grand total was only $12.76 which included a blow to my self-esteem. If the 40-something year old cashier at Trader Joe's cares about what kind of purse I have, then this is a clear sign that he has a passion for something larger than two buck chuck so I can make sense of his comment as a projection on psychological level and not take it personally. Perhaps he was working at Trader Joe's while he bootstrapped his startup. Or maybe he was working at Trader Joe's to have human interaction nights and weekends because all he did was code during the day and try to do Tinder unsuccessfully with his aesthetic and personality challenges.

In this moment of bagging my items and exiting the store, I realized the universe had just sent me my second wake up call for the evening. Obviously, the first wakeup call was the vomit incident. The second one was a bit more subtle and included being insulted by a cashier. I just moved to San Francisco to have my life fall apart. I am single, unemployed, living in a SRO, with a few suitcases, and purse that is also grocery bag. And, I have someone else's vomit on my shoe.

Chapter 24
Pretending

I wiped my feet off thoroughly on the grassy square outside my building. Almost all the vomit was off and felt it was safe to enter. The part of my evening post-Trader Joe's, included indulging in a $1.99 fusilli frozen dinner and a bottle of Trader Joe's own Blanc de Blancs. More relaxed and with an infusion of *joie de vivre*, I took my computer out and checked my email.

It was better in my mind to drink alone right now and avoid corresponding or speaking with anyone I knew. A story came to my mind that Clara told me in Houston. She said before I got to Houston, they used to have weekly happy hours where sometimes things got a little crazy. At Papi's, the same Mexican restaurant that I went to on the first day of my job, they had one happy hour that ended all future happy hours. From what she had said, Greg had drunk a little bit too much and then went back to the office. He emailed Pamela, who was not at the happy hour but still working, to meet him in the conference room. Greg apparently went into the conference room, got naked, and then took the seat closest to the door. When Pamela entered, she saw all of Greg and shrieked which caused Clara, who had to work late to support Pamela, come to the conference room and also saw all of Greg. Pamela grabbed Clara and pushed her out of the room. She then told Greg, "It's over between us. Get yourself together."

Tonight, was different as I didn't have to worry about answering afterhours work emails or worry about any dysfunctional colleagues. I also didn't have to worry about working the next day so I might as well enjoy this moment with my wine. I checked my email and browsed jobs in the evening as a regular habit. I had to keep on applying for jobs because I knew my unemployment was not going to last forever.

People kept on talking about startups and I also had seen many ads for jobs at startups. I didn't know anything about online business or websites and wasn't sure what a startup really was. While I had applied for some jobs at startups, no one ever called me in for an interview. And, some of the startup job postings I saw on Craigslist seemed a bit strange to me. Tonight, one ad on Craigslist advertised a job that epitomized what I didn't get about getting a job here. It read:

I'm a hacker with my own startup and I'm looking for a marketing ninja for beer pong, foosball and cool trips. It's a plus if you know about SEO and social media, but not required. Bonus if you have awesome tattoos. Reply with the answer to the following questions:
1) What is your passion?

2) If you could only pick one video game to play for the rest of your life, which one would it be and why?

I didn't know what a hacker or marketing ninja were and I wasn't sure why beer and games were mentioned in a job posting either. Also, why did it matter if I had tattoos or not? I had an MBA not tattoos. Besides, the first question automatically took me back to getting fired for lack of passion and the second question made no sense to me whatsoever because I don't play video games. I began to make a file and collect screenshots of such postings as there were many. The absolute gems were always found in the "Gigs" section. If an employment lawyer needed to bring in some new clients, the "Gigs" section many times had ads that would make the Equal Employment Opportunity Commission have a field day. After the "Marketing Ninja" ad, I stumbled across an ad worthwhile which read, "Temporary Seasonal Help Wanted ASAP." While it didn't say much about the company or job, I decided to take a gamble and send in my resume for this gig. At least it would be better than nothing.

The next day, my cellphone rang and I answered, "Hi, this is Sierra."

"Hi, Sierra. This is Peggy. I'm calling in response to your resume. Thank you for applying for the holiday help position. We'd like you to come in for an interview tomorrow at 6:00 pm. Are you available to come down to our headquarters near Powell?"

"Yes, sounds great. One question: what company is this for?" I was a little bit hung over from the night before and I didn't really remember applying for this job.

"Oh, we're a startup and you probably never heard about us. We'll tell you more tomorrow after you sign the NDA. I'll send you a confirmation email right now. See you tomorrow," she said hastily as she hung up the phone before I did.

Chapter 25
Startup Daze

The next day I put on my uniform for interviewing I had bought last week. Instead of the formal black suit I had been used to wearing on interviews, I put on a business casual gray belted dress and little black shooties. I would wear my sweater coat that was made for November evenings in San Francisco. My outfit wasn't complete without a bulky scarf around my neck. I thought scarves were only for snowy weather but I learned about the value of a scarf by seeing so many women and men wear them since I moved to San Francisco.

When I arrived at the interview, I was greeted by a few people standing at a table in the lobby. It seemed as though they shared the same closet and the same size. The two guys were wearing black skinny Levi's jeans. One was wearing a fitted gray shirt that had white buttons. The other was wearing a t-shirt that said "RestEZ." I knew this was no band, no tourist destination, no designer tee. It was a startup logo tee. It was moments like these when I really wanted a startup to have some class and style to stop making these dorky, ill-fitting logo t-shirts. In the two months I've been in San Francisco, I've seen a bunch of these branded t-shirts for companies I'd never heard of. What was really bad to me was to see women wearing tight shirts like these to show off their assets. The only place these branded, ill-fitting company t-shirts look good is in the trash, was my conclusion. Deep down at times I thought it was masochistic that the people who were wearing the shirts knew full well how bad they looked but liked it, in some weird way maybe because they were passionate about fitting in.

After I stopped staring at the ugly, branded t-shirt, the guy said a quick hello and then gave me the NDA to sign, first and foremost. It didn't look like a standard NDA as it was three pages long and was pretty descriptive about nothing that I really understood. I didn't understand why I needed to sign this for an interview but the man in the gray shirt said, "Just sign it. It's a standard thing for startups anyways." I scrawled my signature fast on the line and then he gave me my name tag. There was a woman who appeared and she had a Polaroid camera. She snapped my picture as I soon as I put on my name tag.

Past the welcome crew's table, there was another table stacked with about twenty pizza boxes. I grabbed a plate and two slices and sat down in front of the large screen that was set up. To my surprise, no one else was eating pizza. There were cubicles on the sides of the big projector screen and I saw many people still typing away. The funny thing was I still had no idea what company this was or much about the job.

The pizza tasted like it was made from a frozen beige play dough ball that they didn't fully roll out or cook all the way. As I took my third bite to see if I could become accustomed to this taste, I felt a tap on my shoulder.

"Hi. You know that pizza was meant for our dev team and not the temporary holiday help," said an overweight, constipated sounding man with a too small t-shirt that had "The Best Hackathon 2013" on it.

"Oh, sorry. I'm not going to eat this second piece, would you like it?"

"Yes, because our guys are working so hard and we want to make sure we have enough beer and pizza for our team."

This group interview was off to a great start, I thought, as I slid the second piece of cooked play dough pizza off onto the waiting paper plate he held in his hand. He said a quick "thanks" and then rushed off to a hidden cube.

I gracefully slid the half-eaten slice under my chair and grabbed my notebook and pen from my bag. Now, near the podium, a group of four was talking amongst themselves. In the audience, there were about twenty people ranging from 25-45 years old, all with name tags and none with pizza.

"Good evening, everyone. We are going to go ahead and get started," said a very well dressed woman who was wearing a white pressed shirt, with a black blazer and dark denim jeans. She was wearing a turquoise necklace which impressed me even from where I was sitting. I wondered where she got that.

"OK, so many of you have the same questions and we are going to answer them all at once. We are a new startup that is called RestEZ. We've been disrupting the temporary accommodation space since last year and we just raised our Series A round. This holiday season, we are scaling our business like never before. That is where all you come in. We are looking to you to help make our customers happy, contribute to their wellbeing and enhance their safety."

The audience was silent and the soft typing of the surrounding cubicles was the only sound audible.

"As many of you know, San Francisco is a top tourist destination. You were chosen out of thousands of resumes because we believe you have what it takes to offer our clientele a truly special, Bay Area luxury experience with your amazing abilities."

It sounded like a high-end escort service. I was curious if the Human Resources department really chose me out of thousands of applicants to come and be tempted at dinner time by the smell of pizza we weren't allowed to eat and a side of bullshit.

"We are asking you now to get into groups of four or more with the people around you so that one of our team members can sit down with you and tell you more about this job."

The half-eaten piece of pizza underneath my chair was the only thing around me. I gathered my things and migrated to the front of the room and found a group of three. "Hi, I'm Sierra," I said and sat down.

In this group, there was a blonde woman who must have been about forty-five, a skinny Asian guy who was no more than twenty-five and a dark haired man who was around my age. They all said hello. Our attention turned back towards the screen as now there were a number of ice breaker type questions up.

Somewhere in between me taking out another pen from my bag and giving it to the blonde woman, a Nerf arrow hit me in the head. I casually looked up again towards the screen as if nothing happened.

"Here at RestEZ, we work hard and we play hard. So these Nerf guns are one way we decompress. We have them scattered throughout the office. The harder we work, the more we play. And we also have two kegs at all times for all of you to enjoy anytime you want!"

For fear of something I couldn't put my finger on, but something I was also too afraid to admit to myself, I looked down to my notebook. I need a job, not a Nerf arrow to the head. I waited for some response from the audience to what was said and was surprised that all the prospective new hires were silent. It was an awkward silence.

"And, we wanted to let you know that we have a kitchen stocked with all sorts of goodies. We also have bean bags and a PS4 in our game room that you can use, too."

I did a quick check in with myself to make sure I knew who I was and where I was going in life. I am not eight. I do not play video games. I do not shoot Nerf guns. I do not drink beer. I like fancy chocolate, manicures and French wines. I needed a job to pay off my loans, not a fake family, not a preschool, not a night out with the guys. I wondered how the rest of the group was fairing with this startup courting ritual that was so confusing to me.

Again, the crowd was quiet. After all, we didn't know what the job was about or the most important question: how much it paid. The woman stepped away from the podium and another guy in a RestEZ shirt came over to our group.

"Hey, guys. I'm Todd. Let's go through some of these questions so I can get to know you better."

About a half hour dragged with small talk and introductions before it was finally my turn to speak, "Hi, I'm Sierra. I just moved here about two months ago with my old company. Well, I got let go and I'm looking to start a new job as soon as possible. Oh yeah, and I have my MBA and experience with diverse people."

"OK, thank you to all of you who came out tonight. What happens next is that we'll get in touch with you if we decide to move forward with your application. Have a good night," said Todd. My assessment was that he's a likeable guy who wouldn't be that bad to work for.

Chapter 26
Temp Job

The next day, Todd called me with the news that I was one of the "holiday crew" and I would start the following week. Working weekends was mandatory and my unemployment check would be reduced but I really needed to do something until I got a permanent job. This job didn't sound so bad and it paid above minimum wage.

Actually, I was happy to have this temp job and take a break from looking for a full-time job. It would be the best option to stay at my SRO until this job was over in February because I wasn't sure how I would manage looking for a new apartment and full-time job while working a temp job that required me to work on the weekends.

The orientation and start of the job was fun. I liked the diversity of the apartments I got to see and the guests were from all over the world. My job would be to provide customer service and light housekeeping when the temporary guests would depart. I would greet them upon arrival, make sure they knew where they were going next, call taxis if they needed one, etc. After the guest left, I would take an inventory to see that everything was still there, make sure there were no maintenance emergencies, take out the trash and fill out some RestEZ forms.

It all seemed normal and easy enough to do for the first few weeks. Around the second week of

December is when things started to change. There was some legal drama going on about RestEZ being allowed to facilitate all these services in short-term, vacation rentals in San Francisco. Apparently, there was a gray area between hotels and short-term accommodations which ended up also affecting the service providers to short-term accommodations.

To be honest, I didn't really care what was going on as long as I got paid. My relationship with work in general was undergoing so many changes and moreover, I was working at the lowest level of the company in a temporary position. The big decisions were nowhere near my responsibility. I did attend all the meetings about what to do if a landlord or property manager approaches you. I knew I was supposed to call Todd immediately and tell whoever was asking that I was a friend of the renter who just so happened to be required to wear a RestEZ logo t-shirt.

One day, after a charming South African couple left a two-bedroom penthouse in SOMA, I was in the sitting room writing down a few notes. There was a knock on the slightly opened door and as I got up from the couch to answer it, all I saw was a bright light in my face. I immediately thought of when I would watch COPS growing up and seeing the criminals squint when they were caught on camera.

"This is Joe Cortes from KRON4 news. We are doing an investigative report on RestEZ and want to know who you are and why you are trespassing in this unit?"

"Uh, uh, uh" I was literally speechless. I stood there staring at the light and trying to think of something to say. Words escaped me. I felt nauseated and walked back to the couch. I sat down and closed my eyes. It was the only thing I could do to save my retinas. I could still see the bright light imprint on my eye lids.

"CUT!" yelled someone from behind.

"What is your name?" said the same someone and I felt a hand on my shoulder.

It was Joe Cortes showing his human side. As I slowly opened my eyes, I noticed he does wear a lot of makeup. I was trying to figure out what his real skin tone was when I realized what was going on. It took me a few seconds to grab my phone and dial Todd.

In front of the KRON4 news crew with the cameras not rolling, I held the phone to my ear, and waited until the ringing went to the voicemail greeting.

"Todd, please come to the SOMA penthouse now. KRON4 news is here." And I hung up the phone.

"Well, that wasn't so bad, was it?" said the split personality of Joe Cortes, while he flashed an evil, toothy grin.

I didn't say anything else as fifteen minutes turned into thirty. We all waiting in silence for Todd to come to the penthouse

"OK, guys, our man ain't showing up. Looks like we'll be going now. Take care, little lady," said Joe walking out of the door first, followed by the other members of his crew.

After they left, I called Todd again.

"Hey, Sierra. Sorry I got held up here. You know how crazy things can get in a startup. Did everything go OK?" There it was: the casual, laissez-faire, San Francisco attitude.

"Hi, Todd. I'd like to speak with you when I get back to the office."

"Oh, OK, but I'm leaving at 4:00, can you tell me now what happened?"

"Well, you might want to watch the news tonight at 6:00."

"OK, will do. Have a good night!"

I was not sure if he didn't understand my first message or was playing some sort of upper level management game with me. It was the second time I ended up being thrown under the bus of corporate America. I was finishing up my duties at the penthouse. After that I had to stop back at the office and then I could go home.

By the time I made it home it was almost 6:00 pm. I turned on my TV and checked on the KRON4 website to see if they posted anything. Nothing was on the site about me that I could see and the news was just starting.

The news started like it always did with the most depressing crime stories that one could ever imagine. After a story about a boy being killed in a hit and run chase that ended in the arrest of the driver, the announcer said, "We'll be back with our Technology Segment."

I had to wait through a commercial break to see how Joe Cortes was going to affect my life as I knew it. The anxiety was getting to me and I was so nervous I grabbed a bag of tortilla chips to stuff my face while I watched the next chapter of my life unfold.

"San Francisco is home to some of the world's best innovators but some of these innovators are getting it all wrong." The intro to the segment began with shots of some famous Bay Area corporate headquarters including Yahoo!, Google, Salesforce and then a shot of the RestEZ's office.

After the opening sequence, the camera guy got a good shot of the beautiful building lobby I was just at today with the chandelier, white carpet, and white sofa with the orchids on the low glass coffee table. Then, the intro to the story continued with shots of the exterior of the penthouse building.

"Take RestEZ. A Bay Area startup founded by two hacker brothers from Florida out to make their million. It started off as a simple idea to make money in the sharing economy. But now it's turned into Pandora's box that no one can seem to close."

"We visited this luxury condominium complex in the heart of SOMA to uncover what goes on at RestEZ. What we found might surprise you."

Accompanied with Joe's intro of RestEZ, were shots of the lobby and then the elevator doors closing to make some sort of "surprise you" statement. My fifteen minutes of fame began with me opening the door to the penthouse. It was eerily similar to COPS.

"Uh, uh, uh."

"That is all this entry-level employee could say about her work at RestEZ. Instructed to tell us she was a friend of the owner, this employee called her manager who never showed up to make sure the unit and his employee were not in danger. RestEZ not only will enter your apartment, but they won't send help if someone enters your home unannounced."

Did Joe just stick up for me? By Todd not showing up, did he risk jeopardizing the "Bay Area's Top Places To Work" title? This temp job suddenly left a more lasting mark than I could have imagined.

Chapter 27
No Comment

My schedule said that I needed to be in the office the next day from 9:00 am to 3:00 pm. I was so tired that I almost missed getting off at my bus stop. I exited the bus hurriedly at the last second and started walking to RestEZ's headquarters. I got to the office and had to take a minute before entering. So much emotion was bubbling up I decided to get a tea from the café across the street. I knew I'd be a little late but in my mind it was better for me to be late and collect myself than to go into the office and explode.

"Sierra, can you please join me in my office?" said Todd about two minutes after I walked into the main office door.

"Sure," I said standing up, taking a notebook and pen from my desk. I walked behind Todd and kept quiet.

"Please, take a seat," he said as he motioned to the chair closest to the door. After I sat down, the Human Resources director entered and took the chair next to me.

"I think you remember Peggy from the orientation night."

I smiled at Peggy and said hello. She had a folder in her hand and was not wearing the turquoise necklace today. Todd took the seat behind his desk.

"I saw the news last night and so did Peggy. We wanted to thank you for your service with us and give you a month's salary. Today is your last day and we will be escorting you out of the office after you get your things together from your desk."

"Uh, why am I being fired?" I asked, dumbfounded.

"Let's just say we are looking for people who are more passionate about our business and that these people will be the ambassadors for our business, no matter what the situation is."

"I did everything you asked us to do. I said I was a friend of the renter or owner and then I called you. I am not sure I understand all this."

"Thanks, Sierra. Please sign these documents so that we all can move on," said a non-smiling Peggy.

I had no other choice in that moment but to reluctantly sign the documents that were put in front of me. This was not good. My eyes welled up with tears and I could not read the documents although I scrawled my name as best I could under these circumstances. Finally, the last document was signed and I sat back in the chair.

"Sierra, I will escort you to your desk so that you may collect your things. After this is done, I will see to it that you leave the premises. If you return to this office or your desk for any reason, this will be considered trespassing and treated as such. Does that make any sense?"

This time, the use of the question so unduly popular in modern Bay Area English, "does that make any sense?" struck a dissonant chord with me. I hated this question from first time I first heard it until this present moment. The condescending tone coupled with the fact that the asker of this question usually has no emotional intelligence whatsoever tends to leave me wondering if I should explain why this question is rude and offensive. What I typically want to say is that the person doesn't make any sense for asking if they make sense. IF they knew it made sense, then they wouldn't have to put themselves on a pedestal of insecurity for asking if someone understood their nonsense.

"Sounds good," I said with an overwhelming sense of courage coming from somewhere deep inside.

We walked to my desk together, side by side. As we walked, I heard less typing and I saw quite a few people standing around in the center of the office where we had the orientation. I grabbed my things quickly and then looked over to see what was going on. At the center of the group was none other than Joe.

"Can you comment on the recent firing of your employee, Sierra Wellington? Why was the decision made to let Sierra go after our KRON4 exposé?"

Again, the camera with the light flashed on my face and Peggy grabbed my arm firmly to walk me to the front door, and said, "No comment."

Chapter 28
That's What Friends Aren't For

That evening, for the second night in a row, I saw myself on the "Technology Segment." It was truly incredible that I was getting almost my full fifteen minutes of fame spread over a few days courtesy of Joe. The beginning montage was over and he started speaking.

"You may remember this employee from last night. Her name is Sierra Wellington and she got fired today. Fired for following instructions and doing her job. We wanted to know why this happened and went to RestEZ to find out."

There was the front of the office shot, followed by another COPS-esque sequence of walking down the hall with blurred out faces passing by. Then, there was the surprise moment of a close up on my blotchy tear stained face contrasted with the cold demeanor of Peggy replying, "No comment."

"Poor management practices of startups are run of the mill these days. We're going to get to the bottom of this and let you know your rights. We'll be following this story all month and tomorrow we'll have an employment lawyer to answer your questions live," Joe said seated at the main newscaster desk.

For the next hour, I stared at the TV in shock. I was in a semi-catatonic state of disbelief at my life as seen on TV. This was a surreal moment when it wasn't anymore and while I knew this was the second job I got fired from, I was strongly committed to hanging on to my denial as long as possible and as long as I didn't see myself on KRON4 again. My cellphone started to ring.

"Hey, Sierra. How are you? What happened?" It was Jennifer. We hadn't spoken at all since I moved to San Francisco even though I had called and left her about a message a week since I moved. She would text me from time to time telling me how she had so much work to do and started a new relationship that she wanted to focus on. It had been disappointing not to see her or talk to her but now I was relieved she finally called me probably all because she saw me on the news.

"Do you want to grab a drink? I can come to meet you in Russian Hill," I said as if nothing out of the ordinary was happening.

"No, I'm coming to meet you now."

That is why I liked Jennifer. At her best, she was very empathetic and did what she said she would do. At her worst, she is outspoken, loud and self-entitled. This is how I remember her when we were in D.C. I reminded myself that maybe she has changed as I have, too. I wasn't sure how it would be to finally see her in the weird moment of a reunion because I now had some drama that was very public going on in my life.

I went downstairs and saw a cab pull up and Jennifer get out. I opened my building door and gave her a big hug. I was happy to finally see her and have a friend, at least for the present moment. She had changed her hair by now wearing it short above her shoulders but everything else looked the same to me. She signed in with the security officer who was, for once, awake and we went up to my apartment.

"Have you spoken to a lawyer, yet?" she asked, like they must train you to do in law school.

"No and I'm not sure if I will or not. It's so good to finally see you, Jennifer! How are you?"

"We can talk about me later. I think you may not understand what's going on, Sierra. You have to defend yourself and your reputation in this situation. This is San Francisco and if you don't take care of your reputation, you'll never find another job. I don't know why you took that stupid startup job in the first place. And, you still have your boxes at my place."

This was all true and like a good friend, Jennifer was telling me how she saw it and how I wasn't living up to my true potential. The elevator doors opened and we walked to my apartment.

"It's not fair what these startups are doing to people. They are ruining people's lives. This is the second situation that you've been let go and done nothing. Don't you think you should?"

I opened the door and let that question go unanswered as I took a seat in the corner. Jennifer took off her raincoat and put it on the back of the chair in the opposite corner. Jennifer didn't sit down but crouched down near my chair and put her hand on my shoulder.

"What are you doing?" I said confused at the depth this was going to when I just wanted to catch up with her, find out who she was seeing and then go for a drink.

"I'm worried about you, Sierra. Look at you. You got your MBA and then got a great job in Houston. But then how did you go from that to this? This is the second time in less than six months you have gotten let go from a job."

I looked at her and then I looked away. Jennifer went to the other chair and sat down. We both sat in silence for a few minutes.

"Jennifer, you may not know what it's like to keep on living in debt. My parents haven't helped me pay off my student loans or my credit card debt. I know I'm smart and have the MBA to prove it. But I don't know why it has been so hard to find a job and keep a job. You know me, I'm not a bad or lazy person. I guess this is just bad luck or some karma I can't explain. You also know I'm not going to give up. I mean, it's pretty hilarious that I got on TV and was working for two companies that were so messed up. Did I tell you my boss in Houston wanted me to pretend to be his wife when we were on a business trip?"

A loud knock on the door startled both of us as Jennifer went to the door.

"Who is it?" she asked.

"It's Joe with KRON4. Is Sierra available for comment?"

"This is her lawyer and we are not responding to enquires from the media."

I loved and hated Jennifer in moments like this. I wished she would just come up with some magic statement that made me look like the heroine I saw myself after that come-to-Jesus armchair speech. Instead, she gave some key observations which hurt me. I needed her support and not her pointing out my shortcomings.

"Sierra, I think it's best I go now. Call me if you need anything and don't talk to the media." Jennifer said as she grabbed her raincoat and left me sitting in the chair, almost still waiting for her to come back again and say something nice.

Chapter 29
Manboys

I had committed a few weeks prior to volunteering at a startup event that just so happened to be the day after I got fired. For obvious reasons, I didn't really feel like being around anyone. I knew I had "to get out there" to find a real job and I had to use my networking skills to find my next opportunity. Although, emotionally, I just couldn't handle this event tonight after being on the news two days in a row this week. I wondered if anyone would recognize me.

On BART, on my way to the event, I was being punished by the odor of human and animal filth. I put in my earbuds to distract myself as I turned up my music. I also said a little prayer that everyone on BART would know the value of a good shower with soap and stop making people suffer with their stench. Just when I finished the prayer, a strange man pushed his way through the people standing close to the door to enter my car.

"You keep on putting that laptop on your dick and call it a dicktop. It's frying your 2-inch wiener like a hot dog in a campfire. But you like that. Impotent fuckin' geek," said the strange man who was carrying a bag that said "Patient's Belongings" to an unsuspecting, hipster guy who was seated in the reserved seat for handicapped and pregnant people. This hipster guy seemed to be a caricature of trend incarnate with his glasses, full beard and black Levi's and didn't react or even look at the man.

Sparing no lost time, the homeless man did a 180 and pinned a guy against his bike that was supported by the wall of the train.

"And, you with your collapsible bike...it's taking up too much space on this fuckin' train. Shove it up your white hairy ass. Oh no, wait, you'd probably like that too much."

The tirade continued and the strange man did another 180 and bent down to get in the face of an Asian girl, who looked all of fifteen sitting next to the hipster man.

"What about you, Miss Priss with the Hello Kitty shit that exploded all over. You're a freak."

And, with that, the homeless man took out his penis and peed on the girl's Mary Jane shoes. The foul-smelling pee bounced off the black patent leather and started making a pool under the two reserved seats. The saddest thing is that no one was doing anything. After the man was done peeing, it was the Montgomery street station and he zipped up and exited the train. Then, someone used the call box to report, "Uh, some man just urinated in this car."

That incident had to be one of the most blatant displays of adult mental illness I had ever seen. Actually, it was tied with the day a cracked-out girl of about twenty ripped someone's laptop out of their hands at a café and smashed it on the ground. In both situations, no one did anything except stare. I was confused as to why the men present didn't take a step to help. Many people seemed to be zoned out with their phones and almost conditioned to watch and not participate.

Sandwiched in the middle of the car, I didn't have cell reception and I was also about half the size of that man. This man could have been my neighbor at my SRO and I wouldn't have known it. I understood from seeing so many mentally ill people on the streets that there was a big problem with this population and while I wanted to help and overcome my fear, I didn't know how and hadn't seen any examples of what is the right thing to do would be.

What had seemed like a tremendously long ten minute journey to the W Hotel, ended when I walked in the lobby and saw the registration table. I quickly changed my mentality to project confidence and, if all else failed, at least I looked good in my special event black dress. The event was scheduled to take place on four floors of the W with various activities at different levels. I was in charge of signing up people to take part in a sumo wrestling tournament which was set up on the rooftop deck of the hotel.

This volunteer commitment was ridiculous as how could I have a serious conversation or network with people if I had to recruit them to sign up to be sumo wrestlers. I had a two hour shift working at the sumo wrestling ring and thought this was going to be a long two hours because what kind of professional adult would want to be a sumo wrestler at a networking event?

As I stood with the clipboard trying to take this job and myself seriously, I noticed there was a ratio of four men to one woman. And, most of these men looked the same to me with their jeans, tennis shoes and t-shirts. Some had hoodies while others had put on a jacket of some type. No one was waiting to be a sumo wrestler so I spent some time looking at each activity that was set up. I was astonished and never had I seen adults acting like children in a public place. This confirmed what I had seen at RestEZ and heard from other people where companies would have slides, bean bags, toys and video games for their employees to use.

I had also heard about the stereotypical, perpetual Peter Pan man in San Francisco. I could connect Peter Pan men to being products of their environment. The candy, the juvenile color schemes, the brightly colored lunch tray cafeterias, the bus ride to the office all reminded me of endless school days which could equate to the modern-day, Bay Area Neverland.

And now, seeing these manboys, I was super confused about San Francisco and the men that live here. In an attempt to make sense of seeing grown men revert back to childish behavior I was coming to the conclusion that since money did offer freedom and, in this case, perhaps the trend is for well-paid men to choose to be a type of manboy. I took a look at the few men I signed up for the air house and saw them happy in their eight year old comfort zone bouncing around in sumo suites which wasn't all that bad as they weren't hurting anyone.

"Hey, you want to go grab a drink?"

I turned around to see a very attractive, tall, dark haired man standing behind me wearing an actual suit that was pinstriped and a blue tie.

"Yes, I would," I said and left my clipboard and the manboys after only completing a fraction of my volunteer shift.

Chapter 30
American Woman

I had no idea who this handsome, well-dressed man was but I didn't really care. I needed a break from the treadmill of thoughts about manboys, San Francisco and startups, for my own mental health. A drink was an adult thing to do and he wasn't dressed in a sumo suit so I figured he was respectable.

We left the W and headed to a bar. We sat down at the bar and the man started speaking in Spanish to the bartender. I could understand a little but had no idea this was a Spanish place.

"Hi. My name is Cristian. What is your name?"

"Sierra. Sierra Wellington." All of a sudden a wave of something washed over me as I took all of this man's charisma and charm in.

"Sierra. Like a mountain. Hahaha."

"Yes, my parents were hippies. They loved nature. That's how I got my name."

"Nice to meet you, Sierra. Thanks for joining me for a drink."

"My pleasure. I wasn't doing much at that party anyway."

"Why did you go to that party? Is that a typical American event?"

I wasn't quite sure how to answer his questions or who he even was. He could have been anyone from an investor to a bootstrapped hacker trying to get investors. He wasn't dressed like he was boot strapping anything although I couldn't really tell where he was from or much about his motives for this drink.

"Well, to be honest, I am looking for a job and thought that party would be a good place to network. And, no, that is not a typical American event. Well, yes, I mean if you are eight or live in the Bay Area."

A pitcher of sangria arrived and I liked Cristian even more just then.

"Sorry, I don't understand. Can you tell me more? I am not eight, by the way. Haha."

He definitely did not have an American sense of humor but he was laughing at his own jokes which was endearing. His smile was perfect and I found myself wanting to just look at him and not even take the sangria he poured for me.

"It's like this in San Francisco: Many companies will treat the employees like they are kids, around the age of eight. I think that some companies believe that they can either control their employees better if they revert them back to that time in their life or maybe they think that the employees will work better if they have bright colors, bean bags and games at the office. It's my observation. Did you see the sumo ring at the party? That is one example."

I took a slow sip of the sangria to avoid the floating fruit. I did like the fruit a lot but right now, all I cared about was the liquid and not spilling it on myself

"Oh, I see. Where I am from, in Madrid, we don't have these parties for adults who want to be children. But in San Francisco, aren't there many fathers?"

The substitution of fathers for parents had to do with false friends when translating between Spanish to English. This took me so off guard not only because of the literal question of fathers in San Francisco but also how do I explain the manboy, Peter Pan syndrome to a cultured European man? I took a deep breath and looked at Cristian who was focused on listening to me answer this question.

"Well, this is a very complicated question to answer." I paused after saying this and thought how to answer this diplomatically without sounding like a cat lady spinster who's given up on love and devoted her life to speaking feline. Even though on paper, I looked like a hot mess since I got fired twice in four months, I still had some femme fatale in me and wanted to be seen as a sophisticated, successful, American woman who's open to a hot European boyfriend.

"On one hand, San Francisco has a lot of very intelligent, successful people, both men and women. These people tend to put technology and work ahead of a traditional relationship. They use apps and email to communicate all the time but see very little of each other. Maybe you saw when CNN did a special report on the private lives of people in Silicon Valley?"

"No, I didn't. Why is that news?"

"So, here in San Francisco, I think that many people are liberal and have different lifestyles than people in Michigan, where I'm from. For example, I heard about people who have open marriages."

"What is an open marriage really about?"

"You know what I'm going to send you that link to the CNN report. Basically, many people have different lifestyles in San Francisco than other parts of the US and maybe the world, I don't know. Also, there is something called the Peter Pan syndrome here where grown men act like the eight year olds I mentioned before. Like, they avoid responsibility of being married and a father, sometimes they don't get jobs, maybe they live at home, play video games, ride scooters. Really, like they are in a stunted pattern of being a citizen of Neverland – just like Peter Pan."

"Sierra, I'm not sure what you are talking about. Plenty of people that I've seen and talked to here look like adults and act like adults, too. Just look at you."

"Thanks for the compliment, Cristian."

"Do you know what is going on in Madrid now, Sierra? We have something similar. In Spain, we have a crisis that doesn't seem to end. We have very, very high unemployment and we have many people who don't have jobs – especially young people. These people live at home with their fathers until some are in their 30's. It's like what you said about the Peter Pan men, only different because Spain is different, as we say."

After he said this, there was silence as we both looked at each other in the eyes. I didn't know what to do so I did nothing but just stare at this man in front of me who was nothing like anyone I had ever met before.

I thought it was best to leave as soon as possible so I said, "Cristian, I have to go back to my apartment now because BART is going to stop running. "

"OK, Sierra. Will we see each other tomorrow?"

"Sure; if you have time, I mean. I'm going to go to a venture capital event in Palo Alto for startups."

"Can I come to the event? I can drive; I have a rental car."

"Great. Here's my number and I'll RSVP for you. We need to leave at 3:00 pm to beat some of the traffic. Can you please come to pick me up then?"

"Yes. But, I'll need your address. I will send you a text tomorrow. Hasta mañana, Sierra."

Chapter 31
Psycho Tech

I went home after drinks with Cristian and felt like I was on cloud nine. After the past few days of being on the news, getting fired and working at an event where I had to sign people up to wear a sumo suit, meeting Cristian was truly a sign that humanity isn't as messed up as I thought. Before I went to bed, I added a guest to my RSVP for the Palo Alto event.

That night I had a dream that I will never forget. It was so real, I wasn't sure if it really was a dream or part of some show I forgot to turn off before I went to sleep. I dreamt that I got a job at a gaming company that had a game called "Hangry Ants" which was about a group of hungry and angry, gangster ants that try to take over all the ant hills. The ants were so smart they made robot ants as decoys to find ways to the ant hills they wanted to overtake. This game was the number one game across the world and the gaming company called their fans "ants" which was a psychological game to get the "ants" addicted and make the company more money.

As part of my job in the dream, I had to keep track of all the ants in the colony called "the valley." This was like an alternate reality where the members of the community had the same ant picture on their profile and only the name was changed. I kept on loosing track counting until the queen ant who was really my robot boss came up to me, looked at me and was going to eat me but I woke up just in time before that happened.

I sat up in bed from fright. That dream was so far-fetched but rooted in it I understood what it was trying to help me process. The ants were like the people I saw tonight who looked all the same to me. I was insecure about my volunteer role of trying to sign up them up to be sumo wrestlers and keep track of them. But what was most frightening to me was that the queen ant had all the power and she wanted me dead because I kept on messing up. Could the queen ant be representative of my Mom? I knew my Mom was unhappy with my choices but that was her problem.

After this nightmare, it took me two hours to fall back asleep. When I woke up it was already noon and I took my time to get ready for the startup event in Palo Alto. I had to leave that nightmare behind and look my best, not really for the event but for Cristian. I texted him my address and he texted me back that he would pick me up at 3:00 pm as planned.

It was finally 3:00 pm and I went outside my building to wait for Cristian. After ten minutes of waiting, I texted him to see what time he would arrive. No answer. I thought to myself how silly it was to believe that Cristian was actually going to show up. After all, I just met him last night. And, I couldn't find him on LinkedIn to see who he really was. It was now 3:45 pm and Cristian pulled up to my building in a red, Mustang convertible with the top down.

"Hola, Sierra. Do you like my convertible? I rented it because it's California!"

"Hi, Cristian. Yes, nice car. We have to go or we'll never make it there."

I quickly got into the car and directed Cristian where to go. During the car ride, we talked about the Bay Area. I told him more about the event from what I knew and how it was specifically for young startups looking for venture capital funding. These events happened once a month in Palo Alto and tonight's event was geared towards international startups.

"Sierra, why did you want to go to this event, then?"

"The same reason as the last event. I thought it would be a good opportunity to meet startups who need help and that would want to hire an MBA looking to make a career change. Well, to be honest, I just need a job and the more people I meet, the better my chances."

Cristian pulled into the parking lot of the event venue and parked the car. He looked at me and said, "I have an idea. I could use your help in Madrid with my startup, Sierra. We need someone like you: a native English speaker that can help us with marketing and business development."

"Oh, I'm not sure, Cristian. Let's talk about this later and go in."

We went into the event and picked up our nametags. My name was fine but under my name it said "None" where it should have said a company's name. Looking around I saw a couple of porta potties set up in addition to a few food tables that had gummy bears and granola bars out. I also saw a table full of plastic bags that they were giving away to people and I went over there while Cristian went to use a porta pottie.

"Hi, can I please have a bag?"

"Yes, can you tell us a little bit about your company, what is it, 'None'?"

"Oh, it's not really called 'None.' I'm looking for a job that is why I'm here."

"OK, well these bags are for people that have jobs at startups but we have some extra so you can have one, I guess."

"Thanks."

That was brutal. I was ready to go back to my bed. The only good thing was that Cristian was here and I could talk to him. Maybe he really did mean I could work for him or maybe that meant I could be his girlfriend, too. I took a seat to look at what was in the bag only for people who work at startups and saw a bright yellow flyer for a co-working space in San Francisco. If I brought the flyer to this co-working space, I could get a month free. This is exactly what I wanted to do. I would meet people and have somewhere to go during the day.

Cristian found me and took the seat next to mine. We listened to the speaker as well as the pitches then left shortly after to drive back to San Francisco. We both were tired and didn't say much even as Cristian pulled up in front of my building.

"Goodnight, Sierra. Thanks for inviting me to the event. Let's talk soon," he said as he moved forward for what I thought was going to be a kiss but just ended up being a little pat on the shoulder.

"Bye, Cristian. Thanks for driving. Have a good night," I said after he took his arm back and unlocked the doors.

Chapter 32
Adult Daycares

A few days later, I brought my flyer from the startup event to the co-working space. I was determined to focus on my job search and re-organizing my life. Besides, co-working was something I had never tried before and thought it would be a refreshing change to do something new.

From the website, I wanted to believe that co-working was the future of work where solo professionals can find their tribe in the accepting environment of rented desks. Networking, happy hours, comradery were all included in addition to the all you can drink fair trade Costa Rican coffee. Phone rooms for private conversations and conference rooms for meetings were available. Productivity was in every corner of the first floor, former retail space of a department store that went out of business.

Upon entering, I was greeted by a voice, "Hi there! Welcome."

This was not a good start. The ubiquitous "Hi there" has never ceased to annoy and sadden me. A greeting followed by an adverb is plain stupid, informal and impolite. No one's name is there and no one is saying hello to a spot over there. I wondered where the voice that called me an adverb came from as I looked to the left and to the right but didn't see anyone.

155

All of a sudden, I jumped out of my skin and a muffled "AHH" came out of my mouth as someone started tapping on my shoulder.

"Didn't mean to scare you! How can I help you?"

The person standing next to me was wearing a cowboy shirt with button down pockets and belted baggy jeans cuffed to perfection over black Doc Maarten boots. The retro 1950's black industrial looking glasses were the quintessential accessory that highlighted their face.

"Hi. I talked to PJ over the phone about starting today."

"Great. I'm PJ & welcome. We've got this desk reserved for you. The Wi-Fi code is on the board under the coffee of the day. You can put anything you want in the fridge. Let me know if you need something."

"Thanks."

I went to the fridge to put my sandwich inside. Then, I walked over to an empty desk, sat down and was ready to work.

"Yeah, can you believe it? She is only twenty-two and she's an intern at a social media app startup. She was all over me, bro. I took her out for a few drinks and she was so horny. We got a room!"

Who was this talking in the cube next to me? I popped my head over to see an inflamed, acne faced young man with a full beard and green zip hoodie.

Without the protection of an organized Human Resources and PJ was hardly a stand in for an effective Human Resources manager, the downside of co-working was being exposed to these situations that are uncomfortable, I soon realized.

"Oh yeah, she's cute. I'm going to text you a pic. She's got a friend. Maybe we could all go out tomorrow so you could get some, too?"

Assaulted by the lack of self-respect this guy had and his vulgar proposition to another one of his kind made my stomach turn. This was not going to end for the next foreseeable future as I was quickly being exposed to the culture of this co-working space.

I had just gotten there but was so uncomfortable I needed to do some emotionally eating. I made my way back to the fridge to get my sandwich I had brought. In keeping in line of saving money, I set the goal for myself to bring my lunch every day. Mostly, it was going to be a simple hummus and lettuce sandwich. If I had tomatoes or leftover cooked veggies, I would put them in there, too.

When I opened the fridge, I saw there was only half of my sandwich left. I was disgusted. Someone looked at my hummus and lettuce sandwich, then took it out of the refrigerator and used a knife to cut neatly down the center of the wheat bread then put the sandwich back into the Ziploc bag. And, this person put the sandwich back in the same spot that they took it from. This was absurd, ridiculous and abnormal.

PJ came out of nowhere and asked "How's it going?"

"Someone ate my sandwich."

"Oh, are you sure? Maybe someone just moved it."

"Yes. I brought a full sandwich and now I have this," I said as I held up the Ziploc bag with half remaining.

"Did you put your name on it?"

"No."

"Well, there you go. Your name wasn't on it so technically anyone can help themselves to it."

"Thanks for the clarification."

I looked at my poor sandwich and didn't want it after someone's hands, presumably, dirty, cut it in half. Maybe they were trying to be nice by only taking half but it bothered me so much that I didn't even want to eat it. I put a sticker on it after PJ showed me where they lived and instead of putting my name, I put "free." Not that it needed a free sticker but now giving permission to someone seemed like the best thing to do.

The apple I had in my purse was what I would eat now and I went to grab my purse from under the desk. I walked back to the kitchen area and took out my apple to eat. I knew I didn't have more than five dollars in cash in my wallet and not sure if I could use my credit card to buy a sandwich. I took out my wallet to double check if I had miscalculated my cash. Then, I saw that guy in the green hoodie go to the fridge. I watched him as he grabbed the other half of my sandwich.

"Someone left this sandwich and I'm so hungry and hung over from last night. There was no name on it. Sucker."

I looked at this guy and then just got up and walked away without double checking my wallet. I went out of the co-working space and immediately felt better. This was only a small thing and maybe the people will change every day here, I tried to reason with myself. But, if everyone was so successful in San Francisco, why did they need to eat other people's sandwiches?

I went to the corner liquor store that had a small deli two blocks from the co-working space. I knew what I wanted and ordered a hummus and veggie sandwich. I didn't even ask how much it would be but figured it couldn't be more than five dollars.

"That'll be $7.50, miss," the guy said as he put the white wrapped sandwich on the counter.

"Here you go," I said, giving him my American Express card.

He swiped the card, once and then again.

"Miss, your card didn't go through."

"Try this one," I said handing him my Visa that I knew wouldn't go through but maybe my Mom surprised me and made a payment on that one.

Same thing happened as he went to swipe it a third time.

"I think it's your machine. These cards have plenty of room on them," I said blatantly lying through my smile.

"Don't you have $7.50 in cash?"

"No."

"OK, well, it's not our machine so just take it. It's on the house today."

"Thanks." I left in a hurried, bruised ego way but not too embarrassed to take a free sandwich. I was well aware I couldn't pay for it and I tried to blame it on the credit card machine because I was still angry that some inconsiderate person ate my sandwich in the first place.

I walked back to the co-working space with my free sandwich in hand. Entering the space, I saw there was an empty table in the kitchen area. I grabbed the table and sat down. I was so hungry by now I wanted to eat the sandwich, paper and all. But I needed something to drink. I set the sandwich down and walked to the water cooler.

The green hoodie guy was on a roll in the middle of the kitchen with a few other hoodies listening to him saying, "So, it's like life imitating art. Like *Silicon Valley* on HBO where we are building something that's going to help the world and that there are like so many people with money and VC's that want this. Then, we can say no unless they meet our demands. We are living that show. This is why people from all over of the world come here. I'm doing it, bro. I should be on that show!"

After a week at the co-working space, I never went back. It was like a daycare for people I never wanted to see again.

Chapter 33
Shaky Ground

Christmas was a little over a week away and I was getting to the point of five months ago before I moved to Houston. I still was waiting for my big break in San Francisco. I could now barely afford my apartment, student loan payment and other living expenses. I was scrapping by and avoided shopping and going out to eat. My extreme frugality lifestyle was now at the best it had ever been; I only bought things on sale at the grocery store and walked to wherever I needed to go.

Like a band aid that was about to fall off, my false sense of security was something I was well aware of. I did not have enough money to go home for the holidays and did not want my family to rip off my band aid anyway, exposing my failures of the past few months. It would be too painful to talk about all of this in addition to explain why I was still single.

Cristian sent me a message saying he wanted to see me this week before he went back to Madrid. I thought maybe he would bring up me working for him again and I wanted to turn that into a husband and wife startup where a Spanish entrepreneur had fallen in love with his brilliant, American MBA CFO who he met while on a business trip to San Francisco.

I met up with Cristian at the new coffee shop across from my building. I didn't want to ask if he could tell what type of neighborhood he was in. He definitely looked out-of-place being clean shaven and wearing a white shirt, black sport coat and jeans. He was holding a newspaper that he put down on the table.

"Hi, Sierra. How are you?"

The newspaper opened to the front page and I saw a picture of my building there.

"I'm fine. Can I see that please?"

I took the paper and read the headline "Chinese Investor Buys Second SRO." I skimmed the article to learn that my building had been sold last week to the same Chinese investor that Brown and White had worked with to construct the 88-unit luxury building last year. Brown and White was mentioned as well as Steve who had struck a deal with the mayor to expedite the sale and start demolition of the site early next year.

"Sierra, I'm leaving tomorrow and I wanted to talk more seriously with you about coming to work with me in Madrid."

"OK."

"I can't get you a work visa but you can come for three months and see how you like it."

"OK."

"What do you say? You will come and start working with me in January?"

A job in another country working for a man I find incredibly attractive would not solve my financial problems. No, I don't want to work with you, I want to be your wife because I keep on meeting manboys and my life doesn't really have any purpose and the shithole I call home is not going to be there in a few weeks.

"Uh, sure. Look, that's my building and it's going to be demolished. My Spanish is really bad but I need a job and I need to get paid what I would get paid in the US to work for you. If you can buy me a ticket and find me an apartment, I'll think about it."

"Great, Sierra. My family has an extra apartment and it's no problem to buy you a ticket and pay you the salary that you want. I will send you more information and would like your answer before Christmas."

"OK, thanks. I will wait for your email and let you know. Sorry, I'm a bit taken aback by the news about my building."

"Sierra, sometimes you have to swim with the currents of life. I have another meeting across town and need to go now. It was good meeting you while I was here in San Francisco and I hope to see you again in Madrid."

"Bye, Cristian. Have a good trip back home."

Chapter 34
Taking the Right of Way

My experiences in Houston and now San Francisco left me barely treading water and I was running low on money. Cristian might have been the proverbial and cliché knight in shining armor to save my life especially when he said to "swim with the currents of life." I knew that maybe it wasn't exactly the best idea to set romantic expectations but if nothing else, it was a change. The most important consideration was that I had very little to lose at this stage in my life to try to go for another adventure.

I got an email from Cristian outlining the job he wanted me to do for his startup, ParaLlevar. It was a food delivery startup and since I was a native English speaker and had research skills, Cristian proposed I be in charge of business development. My goal would be to secure relationships with hotels, hostels, study abroad programs, expats and universities and get them to order from ParaLlevar for their catering and takeout needs. It sounded like something I could do and it might be fun to be responsible for meeting a goal and helping a young company grow. The best part was Cristian said he would match my US salary.

Analyzing from all angles, making a pro and con list, I decided to call Jennifer. She told me about people that leave the US that don't pay their loans ever. Apparently, many people do this. This option was appealing to me. I wouldn't have a visa to work and I probably couldn't manage to make very many loan payments anyway. I wondered if could stop the interest on my credit cards, too, but if I was going to be making my American salary in Spain where the cost of living was lower, I could probably pay off more than I had been able to in San Francisco.

I knew I couldn't talk to my parents about all of this because they probably would freak out. I wasn't even sure they knew where Spain was. But I needed to talk to someone and thought I would go see Bev from Brooklyn. I went to her apartment and knocked.

"Hi, honey. How are you?" she asked as she opened the door.

"Hi, Bev. I met you a few weeks ago in the kitchen and wanted to talk to you about a decision I have to make."

"Sure. You can't come in because my place is messy but let's go to the lobby to talk."

We went down to the lobby talking about the weather and took our seat on a couch near a window.

"Honey, you know that this building is going to be torn down by the Chinese, don't you?"

"Yes. What will you do?"

"I'm not sure. They said they could move some of us old timers to another SRO but we haven't heard anything yet. What about you? You are young you can do so many things."

"Bev, you know I'm not really sure that I want to stay in San Francisco."

"Where do you want to go?"

"I was thinking of going to Madrid."

She looked at me and said, "You've only got nine lives, kiddo, so do it before it's too late."

"Thanks, Bev. How do I tell my family this? They want different things for me."

"Look, honey, you keep living your life for other people your soul is going to die. That's not life. I'm from Brooklyn where I had to be tough to survive. I did it and I did what I wanted to stay true to me. Life has twists and turns but if it doesn't kill you...."

"It makes you stronger..."

"No, it doesn't kill you. Tell your family it's time they get to know you and it doesn't take away from who you are or your relationship with them."

"Thanks, Bev."

"Honey, I got to have lunch. You want a Spam sandwich?"

"No, thanks. I think I'll go call my parents and tell them I'm going to Madrid."

As not to lose the courage that Bev had infused in me, I went to my room and dialed Detroit.

"Hi, Mom. It's Sierra."

"Hi, Sierra. Why are you calling me in the middle of the day? Something happen at work?"

"I don't really want to talk about work because I'm still looking for something that will be a good fit."

"Well, you know you can't always get what you want. And, you have to work hard to make it a good fit, you know. I think you need to keep this job at least for one or two years then you'll have something good to put on your resume or until you find someone to marry you. Everyone is asking if you are coming home for Christmas."

"You know, Mom, I didn't tell you but I actually got fired, not once but twice from jobs. I'm so frustrated trying to do everything I'm supposed to and I'm not even living my life. Some Chinese investor bought my apartment building and I won't have a place to live in a couple of weeks."

"So, you want money, don't you? Or you are going to come back to Detroit? Sierra, you know we're going to charge you rent if you end up here. I don't know why you can't find a nice man to take care of you."

"No, Mom, I'm not moving back to Detroit and I'm not coming home for Christmas. It's my turn to travel and live my life. I'm going to work for a Spanish entrepreneur in Madrid. And, I really don't care what everyone thinks. I have the right of way here to do what I want with my life."